A Animal Spirit

Spells, Sorcery, and Symbols From the Wild

Patricia Telesco

and

Rowan Hall

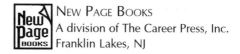

NEW PAGE BOOKS
A division of The Career Press, Inc.
Franklin Lakes, NJ

ANIMAL SPIRIT
Edited by Kristen Mohn
Typeset by Eileen Dow Munson
Cover design by Cheryl Cohan Finbow
Printed in the U.S.A. by Book-mart Press

To order this title, please call toll-free 1-800-CAREER-1 (NJ and Canada: 201-848-0310) to order using VISA or MasterCard, or for further information on books from Career Press.

The Career Press, Inc., 3 Tice Road, PO Box 687,
Franklin Lakes, NJ 07417
www.careerpress.com
www.newpagebooks.com

Library of Congress Cataloging-in-Publication Data

Telesco, Patricia, 1960-
    Animal spirit : spells, sorcery, and symbols from the wild / by Patricia Telesco and
Rowan Hall.
      p. cm.
    Includes bibliographical references (p.) and index.
    ISBN 1-56414-594-8 (pbk.)
      1. Animals—Miscellanea. 2. Magic. I. Hall, Rowan. II. Title.

BF1623.A55 T445 2002
133.4'3—dc21

2002069346

This book is fondly dedicated to my incredible familiar Shaman, and his household companions: Cedar, Kismet, Motzart, Sesi, Amy, and Dax.

For Zane, who saw my potential as a human being and supported me long before I even had a clue as to who I truly was or my Path. Your friendship, belief, and kindness over the years and many miles has been a constant source of comfort and joy. I don't say it enough: thank you.

—Trish Telesco

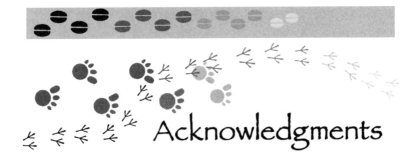

Acknowledgments

My gracious thanks go to my coauthor and members of her family who provided the necessary scientific information to give this book solid foundations. Thanks also to New Page for allowing us to venture into this wild territory and explore so much!

—Trish Telesco

I would like to thank the Universe for this wonderful life, my ancestors for all of their advice, and my family/phamily for loving me despite my quirks! It really is ALL GOOD!

—Rowan Hall

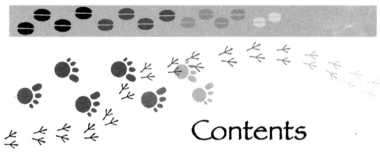

Contents

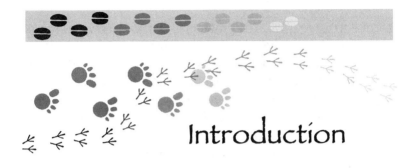

Introduction

Every animal knows more than you do.
—Native American proverb

Feeling bearish? Pecking at your food like a bird? Does someone you know have cat-like balance and always land on their feet? These three questions demonstrate how animals have influenced our language in very concrete and noticeable ways, even if we don't recognize that connection very often. *Animal Spirit* builds on that connection, taking it one step further to show Nature's influence on (and subsequent applications in) modern metaphysical traditions.

Consider for a moment how the wonders of the Earth often reach up to touch us in gentle ways—ways that, at first, may seem insignificant—the nudge of a cat or dog's paw, the flight of a bird overhead, the rummaging of a squirrel in Spring. All of these moments, and others like them, can become potent catalysts for magick if we remain open to them. The key is learning to think and *look* at things a little differently.

Magickal traditions teach that the world is filled with symbols and energy. Within this realm we discover a wealth of patterns and power, each of which holds tremendous potential for modern spiritual pursuits. Animals are an important part of this natural treasure trove. The problem is that, until now, few books have been written that successfully marry science with spirituality and reveal the animal kingdom in all its facets with actual habitats, real behaviors, and common traits to consider in rounding out our knowledge and methods. *Animal Spirit* resolves this by combining sound animal biology with metaphysics.

Now, before that idea scares you off, trust us when we tell you that observing and learning from our animal cohabits is a very ancient and honorable art that nearly anyone can digest. In ancient times, the Shamans and wise people were those who looked for, and listened to, the stories of animal spirits, trusting fully that the Great Spirit left a mark in every part of Nature. Whatever these wise people determined during such spiritual exploits they, in turn, committed to memory and then passed it down via oral and written traditions over the generations so the wisdom of the wild would not be lost.

Any student of metaphysics will tell you that this animal wisdom is still very worthy of our attention. From spirit animals that guide and teach us on our Path, to creatures that appear as portents in our waking and sleeping, the wild world always has been, and should be, a part of walking the Path of Beauty. We need Nature and her creatures because the Earth is our classroom. As humankind lost touch with the Earth's cornerstone in the concrete jungle, we also lost touch with significant aspects of our spirits and our magick. That need not be a trend that continues.

Even as pavement surrounds, we are still part of the Earth and Nature. This planet is a sacred space, and spiritually aware people have a duty to honor it as such. We need to touch again the animal spirit that exists in us and throughout the Universe. Additionally, it is also our duty to treasure and safeguard the efforts of our forbearers in nurturing the secrets of animal magick and keeping them alive for future generations.

Thus, *Animal Spirit* begins at our spiritual roots—with the global history and lore of the animal kingdom. Here, we pause for a moment and take a worldwide tour that illustrates how common myths and superstitions shape animal symbols, signs, and applications in magick to this day. We will also review animal magick as both a method that could be applied to your present practices, or an actual Path unto itself.

Building on that foundation, *Animal Spirit* then brings the scientific element to bear on our exploration. Nature has both beauty and fury: animals can be fun and whimsical or fierce and protective. All of these energies are important to our understanding and use of animal magick. For example, if you're calling on the Otter's power to encourage playfulness, it helps to know that brother Otter can also be snippy. This could result in playtime that becomes rough or emotionally piercing. Brother Otter, being part of the natural world, came with both his positive and negative attributes. To be responsible, aware, and adept, we must know both attributes before invoking such spiritual aid.

Next we come to the proverbial "lion's share" of the book (forgive the pun). Here you get to explore animals as harbingers and signs of things to come. You will also find sound spells and charms that either use animal symbolism somehow or those aimed at protecting and caring for our animal companions.

Taking things one paw further, we will outline the use of animal emblems in the sacred space as Guardians and talk about ways to invite that power. We will also consider the influence of celestial animals in our lives through astrology, combine animal magick with feng shui to improve the vibrations in our living and working spaces, look at celebrations and holidays where animals are key figures in the festivities, and discuss the sacred animals of gods or goddesses around the world.

This variety is one of the fantastic attributes of animal magick. It mixes and mingles beautifully with so many other methods from candlelit spells and herbalism to full formal rituals. We have a long history of animal magick to thank for this flexibility, and the ongoing efforts of modern eco-spirituality advocates who remind us of its renewed importance to our civilization as a whole. If we do not get to know Earth and its inhabitants, we can't respect and cherish their importance. And if we don't respect and cherish this gift called Earth, human-kind could very well find itself on the endangered species list.

As you meander through the pages of this book, it is our hope that you will learn to honor, respect, listen to, and speak to animals in a whole new way. As you do, you will find that your magickal experiences are raised to whole new levels of understanding and being, because we, too, are animals. Let Nature's citizens become teachers, dream guides, helpmates, and fellow travelers on your Path. Allow them to help you reclaim some of the magick that's been lost by reawakening yourself to Earth, self, and to all the magickal possibilities that happen when these two work cooperatively together.

Live free and blessed be.

Chapter 1

What Is Animal Magick?

*We must protect the forests for our children,
grandchildren and children yet to be born. We
must protect the forests for those who can't
speak for themselves such as the birds, animals,
fish and trees.*

—Hereditary Chief Edward Moody

Animal magick can be considered either part of one's sacred wheel or a Path unto itself as surely as crystal magick, Celtic magick, or any other thematic metaphysical pursuit can. But what constitutes animal magick? How does someone know if it's right for them? How do you add it to your present spiritual pursuits and practice it responsibly?

These are not easy questions, but ones that this chapter will try to address. We should note at this juncture, however, that animal magick certainly isn't limited to what we normally think of as an animal! There are insects, amphibians, fish, and so forth. For the purpose of this book, we will be using this broadened definition, and we'll focus on the most common animals appearing in global magickal traditions. To cover them all would require a set of encyclopedias!

13

Also, please bear in mind that what we're presenting here is a broad overview, not a carved-in-stone gospel. Like all magickal paths, the way each person walks-the-walk in animal magick is going to be slightly different. As you read, consider what kinds of personal touches you'd like to bring to this methodology to make it truly meaningful and powerful for your daily life. In fact, we recommend that you get a journal in which you can make notes about your impressions, feelings, successful utilization of exercises, and those things that you found really appealing to your higher senses. This type of journal can become a Natural Book of Shadows in the future, to which you can turn again and again for ideas and insights.

Furry Folklore and Myth

We begin our exploration of animal magick by turning back the pages of time for a moment. The history and lore of animals influences every corner of our lives and it certainly affects the way their symbolic values were (and are) used in spiritual contexts. Consider for a moment the expression "I have a frog in my throat." This colorful description came into being because Shamans used frogs to cure throat problems. The patient would be asked to hold the frog in his mouth for a moment (to transfer the disease) then remove it and let the creature hop away with the cold in tow. This bit of ancient folklore was handed down from generation to generation until the practice transformed into an old saying, the origin of which few understood. Nonetheless, frogs continue to have metaphysical associations with health and healing as part of their virtues.

Shamans and ancient priests and priestesses not only employed animals in spells and rituals, but they also often donned the guise of various creatures. We know this because cave paintings dating back to prehistoric times featured people wearing bestial masks. Why did they do this? There could be one of several reasons. Perhaps the person was simply trying to camouflage himself for greater safety in the wild. Perhaps he was

doing some type of personal ritual (akin to prehunting prepa-
rations in which many hunters still engage), or perhaps he was
a Shaman doing a ritual for the whole tribe, namely, working
magick for a successful hunt. In the latter instance, dressing as
a specific creature was believed to honor the spirit of that animal, and endow the Shaman with the creature's attributes.

On a slightly different level, the psychological effects of
costuming on ritual participants shouldn't be underestimated.
Instead of seeing someone who was always around the village,
and who may or may not have inspired much awe, the tribe
would come face-to-face with an amazing animal spirit, dancing, singing, and raising energy. This particular practice is still
very viable for those wishing to commune with animal spirits,
particularly power animals and guides.

In addition to the tribal fire and the Shaman's hut, another
place animals frequently appeared was the sacred altar. Egyptians, Africans, the early Hebrews, and many more cultures
provided animals as offerings to the Divine. In fact, it is probably safe to say that most ancient religions practiced some
type of animal sacrifice. Not surprisingly, the most common
offerings were those from food-providing creatures, the feeling being that such creatures represented greater value, and
therefore, would make the god or goddess happier and more
inclined to act quickly.

We should mention at this juncture that animal offerings
and sacrifices took two forms. One would be only for the god
or goddess, meaning that after the ritual was over, the animal's
parts might be put in nearby woods and left to Nature's way.
The other form is that of sharing, meaning that either a person
gave part of a daily meal to the altar, or that they partook of
the animal's meat after sacrifice.

This second type of offering was rarely wasted in any way.
Every part of the creature was used somehow, whether to feed
the priests and priestesses of the temple (it was certainly

blessed!) or for making implements. Wastefulness was considered a terrible disservice to the animal's spirit (even an insult to Nature as a whole). One of the neatest modern applications of this idea Trish has seen is a friend of hers who collects roadkill. Now, before you say *ewwwww*, you should know that she properly cleans it, prepares it, then makes the skins into medicine pouches for people. She feels that in this manner the animal's magick is being reclaimed, honored, and put to good use instead of just being left by the roadside.

The Horse. Let's look at some more specific animals, beginning with one of the most important to early people: the horse. Horses provided transportation and much needed help in an agrarian community. But how is it that horseshoes came to represent good luck? Well, it's quite possible that because the horse was sacred to Thor (as was iron), and the ancient northern people are thought to have first put shoes on their horses, so doing was a way to invoke Thor's blessings (for both creature and rider). Thus, horseshoes continue to be a lucky item to this day.

The Donkey. Another working animal, the donkey, obtained most of its symbolic value simply by observation. Not being a terribly bright creature, and prone to slow (but steady) movement, donkeys became a symbol for patience or obstinace (depending on the mood of the moment). This is how we come by phrases such as "stubborn as a mule" and "mule headed." The markings on a donkey's back purportedly originated with Balaam, who, in the book of Numbers, struck his ass en route to Moab. The mark remained on the creature to remind Balaam of his cruelty, and remind all people to be kinder to "dumb animals." Magickally speaking, Trish likes to use this creature's image when she needs to move slowly, but without deviating, through a situation or toward a goal.

Other Farm Animals. Not surprisingly, many other farm animals appear in global lore. The cow and bull are prime examples. Cows represented the Moon Goddess in Egypt, and were aspects of Astarte and Ishtar in Syrian traditions. Hera took the form of a cow in Greece; Celtic and Scandinavian stories tell of nourishing cows, some of which feed entire communities; and cows are still sacred in India.

Bulls were one of the most predominant animals offered to gods and goddesses, having been revered for its usefulness, power, strength, and virility. Many sky and sun gods have th ebull as an attribute. This connection was strong enough in Sumerian tradition that thunder and lightning were once thought to be produced by heavenly bulls stomping, which would be followed by a nourishing rain that made the Earth abundant. In the sacred space, bulls retain their masculine overtones along with the characteristics of sexual potency, stamina, and the ego.

The Goat. Then there is the poor goat. Because Pan got kicked out of heavenly spaces by the new Christian God, his sacred animal ended up being a symbol for evil. Oddly enough, at one time carrying a goat's foot or beard hairs were talismans to protect the bearer from evil. Thankfully, among Neo-Pagans Pan is still a respectable persona, and the goat maintains the god's qualities of fertility and vitality. By the way, Pan wasn't the only old god or goddess who liked goats. Marduk (Sumeria), Artemis (Greece), Azazel (Semetic), Thor (Scandinavia), Yang Ching (China), and Agni (Vedic) all had goat companions or attributes. There is more on divine pets in Appendix B.

Birds. What about birds? We know that the ancient Greeks, Hittites, and Romans "winged it" by creating divinatory systems based on birds, to the point where the word "auspice" once meant "observer of birds"—but why? Quite simply, the bird's power of flight became associated with the soul moving toward heaven or the next life. Additionally, their ability to move through the sky made birds a likely messenger to and from the gods. This was the case so often that many global myths about birds include at least one alluding to a bird laying the cosmic egg from which all things came into being, and have another that talk about a bird aiding a great hero in his quest.

The Rooster. In particular, our morning wake-up call—the rooster or cock—seems to be a very popular chap. Because the song of this bird greets the dawn it has come to represent readiness, alertness, and being awake. In turn, a cock crowing at an inauspicious time, such as midnight, would portend terrible things (death, war, etc.). Bear in mind that the color of a cock was also important in the scheme of things. Egyptians sacrificed yellow ones to Anubis, while among the Greeks a white one was sacred to Athene. And it seems that many cocks had cushy residences being housed in the temples of Hebe (Rome), and Mithras (Persia). Among the Chinese, cocks symbolize bravery and devotion. In Japan, an image of the cock calls practitioners of Shinto to prayer. Finally, in Hebrew tradition a cock and a hen preceded a bridal couple to insure their fertility.

The Fish. Speaking of symbols of fertility, perhaps the most prevalent animal symbol used in the ancient world was that of the fish. Fish come from the primordial Element of Water, to which humankind turned for both drink and food in abundance. Nearly all oceanic or sea-side gods and goddesses, not to mention a fair number of lunar ones, accepted fish as offerings or presided over this creature. Three fishes united by one head represented triune deities in Egypt, India, Mesopotamia, Persia, France, and Burma.

Buddhist myth tells us that fish symbolize the Law, while Hindu stories say that Vishnu's first incarnation was as a fish that saved humankind from the flood. Syrians worshipped fish (and thus would not eat them); the Torah portrays them as devoted; and in Greco-Roman traditions, fish were strongly associated with love goddesses. Not surprisingly, Witches still consider fish a "love" and passion food, and apply this symbol to magick aimed at manifesting fertility, abundance, and providence.

The Bear. Moving from sea to land, let's take a look at the myth, lore, and magick of forest animals. While it's hard to single out a couple, it would seem that bears, deer (specifically stags), and rabbits figure heavily because varieties of all three span a large part of the world. Starting with bears, here we find one of the oldest representations of death and rebirth because of the bear's hibernation cycle. It was also one of the first totemic cult animals because of its ferocity and power. Shamans were said to ride through the astral world on the backs of bears, and some tribal cultures looked at bears as an ancestral spirit. Magickally, bears continue to manifest the energy for overcoming, strength, astral travel, healing, courage, and new beginnings.

The Deer and the Stag. As for the deer and stag, these sure-footed path-finders teach us the ways of the gods, and take part in many mythic cycles such as that of the White Hart of the Celts. In these stories, the deer comes to a hero (or fool) and leads him through the most difficult part of the forest. While deer have strong feminine overtones, the stag is completely male with solar characteristics. Stags are virile watchers of the woods, guardians, and warriors. Metaphysically speaking, the deer's symbolism remains that of swift agility and gentility while the stag is the god aspect and an image that reconnects us to the land.

The Hare and the Rabbit. It seems the myths and superstitions about hares and rabbits are as plentiful as their young. The Chinese revere hares as a symbol of ultimate yin (feminine) power and longevity. Thus, when a hare appeared unexpectedly in this part of the world, people took it as an omen. Specifically, red hares brought prosperity and peace, while black ones portended success and luck.

In other parts of the world, the hare became either a lunar or earthly symbol. For example, in Mexico, South Africa, and Asia, the proverbial man in the moon was not a man at all, but a hare! Because of the hare's obvious reproductive ability, the emblematic value of fecundity and passion were rightfully ascribed, as well as a connection with gods and goddesses known for these energies such as Eros, Aphrodite, and Cupid. Additionally, the hare's fairly deft speed provided a secondary association as a messenger animal for Hemes/Mercury.

The Spring holiday (holy day) of Easter owes its name to the Teutonic lunar goddess Esotra. This goddess bore the head of a hare. Her festival was celebrated during a full moon in Spring to honor the Earth's emerging fertility. According to this story, it is the hare that laid the first Esotra (Easter) egg that begets life anew; so that is why we have the Easter bunny delivering eggs to this day.

The Snake. Among the reptile clan's tales, one of the predominant creatures is the snake. Depending on the era and setting, snakes have been loved or hated, but they rarely have neutral symbolism. Because of its closeness to the Earth, many people connect snakes with the Earth's fertility and/or the underworld, which, in earlier times, was simply a place for the dead, not for demons or evil-doers. The shedding of its skin provides an obvious emblem of renewal and health. Greeks kept pet snakes to appease healing gods, which is how it comes to appear on Hermes' staff.

Despite these positive associations, snakes and serpents were also connected with death, evil, the moral antagonist, temptation, and many other negative attributes. Medusa bore a head of snakes; Hebrews regarded them as unclean; and in Norse mythology, a snake floods the world with venom at the world's end. Joseph Campbell, an American writer who focused on mythology and comparative religion, noted this interesting polarity about snakes, saying that opposites seem to come together in the human consciousness when pondering this creature. With this in mind, spiritually speaking, the snake makes a good figure on which to focus for symmetry and for understanding our own shadows.

The Crocodile. Another interesting member of this group is the crocodile. Crocodiles appear throughout the stories of Egypt, not surprisingly considering the Nile's abundance of them! The only problem is figuring out the crocodile's symbolic value. Because it was associated with sunrise and Sebek (a crocodile-headed god), there are positive connections with the Pharaoh and protection. On the other hand, Typhon, various faces of evil, and the foe of Horus all bore this image! This type of dichotomy is nearly universal, making the crocodile a difficult creature to use magickally.

Insects. And what's all the buzz about insects? While we might not think that insects would be very prevalent to folklore, superstition, and myth (simply because we see them as a nuisance) they certainly had significant roles. Bees and butterflies both appear again and again. Bees have always been admired, because they are connected with honey. Their traditional and continued magickal symbolism is that of order, good work ethics, swiftness, creativity, and purity. Bees purportedly came from Paradise unchanged, and they can travel between the worlds with messages easily. Additionally, several important divine figures are connected with this insect, including Vishnu (one of whose avatars has a blue bee on his forehead); the Egyptian sun god Ra, whose tears become bees; and Demeter in Greece, known as the Mother bee. In Native American traditions the bee represents the community and how to work for the good of all.

The Butterfly. Butterflies, due to their beauty and grace and their natural life cycle, came to represent the soul's journey from life to life. In China they represent immortality, joy, and marital bliss, and Greeks followed suit, perceiving butterflies as a sign of longevity and pleasure. Butterfly-filled winds announce Spring's arrival, bringing hope on their wings, then they disappear again when the Earth sleeps. Butterfly-styled dances in several cultures recount this story and liken it to our spiritual quest. Neo-Pagans keep that tradition alive, considering the butterfly one of the ultimate emblems of transformative power.

The Dog. Moving to domestic animals, how did "man's best friend" get that reputation? Well, certainly part of it comes out of a dog's personality, but there's more to it than that. Folklore tells us that dogs can see ghosts, sense oncoming death or disaster, and warn of storms. As the saying goes, "dogs always know!"

The modern mystical values for dogs have not changed, by the way. They still represent keen second sight, weather magick, and loyalty.

The Cat. Okay, we know cat lovers are waiting for their due regard here! The lore of cats stretches all the way back to Egyptian temples where the goddess Bast was known for her playfulness, health, dancing talents, love of pleasure, and fertility. Bast bore a cat's head, so it's not surprising that her sacred animal would be as light-of-foot and fancy-free as the goddess herself. In fact, Bast's graceful and balanced movements may have contributed to the idea that cats always land on their feet (which is actually a myth, by the way).

One interesting bit of cat lore centers on the black cat. In this case it's not so much the feline, but his or her color that seems to dictate the superstition. One crossing your path, for example, is bad luck, while petting a black cat is good luck. If we consider the symbolic value of something walking before us (which is more dominant) versus petting (which is a symbol of acceptance) this apparent contradiction begins to make more sense. We see this dichotomy with other creatures too, such as the rabbit, where if it crosses your path it is a negative sign, but carrying its foot brings luck. Be that as it may, the cat's magickal value retains the Egyptian influences with attributes such as longevity, balance, and prosperity.

Mythological Beasts. Finally, not all animals that appear in lore come directly from Nature. Mythological beasts and imaginative creatures such as unicorns, dragons, and griffins litter the world's most amazing and wonderful stories. And some of these beasts have natural cousins from which their mythology springs (at least in part). Take the dragon, who is called the serpent with wings. In areas where snakes had positive attributes, so, too, did the dragon (Egypt, China, Japan, Rome). Yet among Christians it is typically a negative emblem, because the snake was the tempter in Eden (thus dragons also became a symbol for treachery and heresy). We consider the dragon a good image to focus upon when pondering the great mysteries, or when we need a little "ancient wisdom" to help our Path along.

Bear in mind that while we cannot prove such things ever existed, these animals have a role to play in animal magick, too. For one, these are the animals of our dreams, which means they have some archetypal qualities that we should not overlook. Secondly, they remind us that there is more to the world than meets the eye, something no spiritual being should ever forget.

Philosophy and Ethics

Animal magick is part of a larger category of metaphysics called wild magick, which covers a wide spiritual spectrum. In this broad category we find Druids, cunning folk, Shamans, Earth Mages, green Witches, and even the proverbial New Age "tree hugger." The thing that draws all these people together is a love of, and reverence for, the natural world and all its potential magick.

Ethically and philosophically speaking, anyone practicing a form of wild magick has similar goals. They strive to:

1. Protect Earth and Nature's resources.

2. Give back to Earth when their arts require something from the Earth (such as replacing a harvested plant with a seedling).

3. Improve their understanding of Nature's voice, symbols, and lessons.

4. See the divine imprint in Nature, and honor that pattern in the way natural items are used magickally.

5. Perceive Nature as a spiritual tool for personal or planetary transformation.

6. Educate others (within and without the magickal community) on the resource Nature represents, thereby aiding to preserve it.

7. Commune with Nature and develop a rapport with Nature spirits.

8. Promote the sacredness of Earth as a living, breathing thing.

Taking each of these points separately, let's start at the top. If you love something, you want to protect it. If we are going to apply Earth's symbols and resources to our magick, we better be willing to defend both. After all, how can one appreciate the deepest symbolic value of a bird in flight if you have never seen one?

Building on that protection and respect, it only makes sense that we would wish to give back from that which we have gathered. There are many little tricks of the trade we can learn from our ancestors (or use to inspire ideas of our own) along these lines. Romans often danced the land, put up garland, and made offerings of grain and wine to the soil, for example. Victorian apple farmers used to give their trees offerings of cider. Other old-time gardeners always put a seedling or a new plant in where one had died or been taken out (if they did not, that plant got turned into the soil for nourishment).

Applying this history isn't that difficult. We know many Pagans who carry a small bundle of herbs or crystals for those occasions when the Earth gifts them with something special. They take out one item from that bundle and leave it on the ground where they picked up Earth's treasure. It seems a very simple gesture, but it's important because it keeps us aware of reciprocity and responsibility, two ethical considerations all animal magicians prize.

As we protect and honor the Earth, it's not surprising that points three and four come of their own accord. Our understanding of Nature's voice, a deeper comprehension of her symbols, and thankfulness for her lessons follows on the heels of courteous attendance. The closer we observe, and the more we open ourselves to truly understanding what we're seeing, we begin to get a glimpse of something far greater in Nature's patterns. We get a peek at the fingerprint of the Universe itself, the prototype pattern that spans all space and time.

Needless to say, discovering this divine imprint is a transformational moment for most of us. The awareness that a rock, a star, a rabbit, a flea, and humankind are all interconnected in time, space, and sacredness really rattles the human egocentric foundations. Whereas before we may have been a little lax about picking up a stray piece of litter or recycling, those actions begin taking on far greater meaning. Suddenly, one's actions or inactions don't just affect self or family. They affect the world, and by extension, touch the whole Universe.

Having put away our tunnel vision and rose-colored glasses in step four, we can then begin applying animal magick as a tool for personal and planetary change. On a personal level, there is so much that animals can teach us (we are, after all, animals ourselves—we just like to think otherwise!). Consider this: Animals know how to read the natural world's signs, how to respond instinctively without second-guessing, how to forage for necessities, and much more. Yes, these are all part of the animal's normal behaviors, which leads us to wonder what normal human behavior would be if we didn't constantly push aside the wild within. Would we, too, learn to read Nature's signals, trust our instincts, and recognize what is truly a necessity versus a "want"? We think so.

Globally, animal magick has a couple levels to consider. First, as we ponder the animal symbols and beliefs of other cultures, our understanding of that culture improves. Symbolism is like a universal language. It allows us to translate the experience and mythology of various peoples so we better comprehend the meaning behind them outside their traditional framework. With that comprehension we begin connecting with the unique members of our human herd a new way—a way that envisions one world, honors our similarities, and celebrates our diversity.

Second, the energy manifested through animal magick is like any other metaphysical method in that it has no limits as to how far it can reach. If you want your efforts to be global—they can be global. If you want to touch the stars—reach out that paw! If you trust in what you're doing, if it's meaningful to you, the potential is endless.

Speaking of reaching out, that brings us to the sixth spoke on our sacred wheel: community education. It is one thing to practice a Path, and another altogether to share that vision with others. Humans are tribal by their nature, and in a tribe knowledge and wisdom beg to be shared. Unfortunately, much of the information about animal magick was lost due to technological growth and societal upheavals. Now that we're finally revisiting this practice, wild Witches don't want what we rediscover to disappear again. The best defense against this is to make ourselves available as a resource to others who desire to learn more. By so doing, we also inspire greater Earth-awareness in others, some of whom may become wild Witches themselves, and others of whom may work toward protecting the environment in more worldly ways.

It stands to reason that in order to teach others, we must also teach ourselves. There are a multitude of animals in this world with an equal amount of folklore, myth, and magick with which they're associated. It is no small task to embark on the conscious learning process. And then there's the intuitive learning process, too. This entails developing a sound rapport and relationship with Nature spirits. We'll talk more about how to accomplish this in Chapter 9, but suffice it to say that going to the source (animal and natural spirits) is always the best way to research and learn! Nonetheless, even as you wouldn't just walk up to an unknown college professor's door and start asking questions, it would be just as rude to impose ourselves on these beings without getting to know them first! Courtesy and consideration go a long way in magick and life.

Finally, it is very important that a wild Witch promote and support the Earth's sacredness. This is as much a point of action as it is a way of thinking and being. If we are taking our cue from Nature, and tapping her storehouse of wonders as a means of raising and directing energy, our footsteps through this world must be gentle and thoughtful, or we're not walking our path ethically (nor are we doing so for the good of all). How do you accomplish this? By changing the way you handle those "close encounters" with animals (and all of Nature).

Is It for You?

If you're reading this book it's highly likely that you've already been bitten by the Nature bug. Nonetheless, it's important to pause for a moment and ask yourself: *Is wild magick really for me?* Not all Paths are meant for all people, and we would be serving no one by encouraging you to try on a proverbial shoe that's the wrong size or style!

Determining a direction in one's spirituality should always be a well-considered moment of thoughtfulness. To help you at this juncture, please consider the following questions, answering them honestly:

🗡 When you think of taking a walk in the woods or in other natural locations, how does that make you feel? Are you excited or energized by the notion?

🗡 When you are in a natural setting, does it distract you from your spiritual pursuits or direct your attention even more strongly that way?

🗡 Do you find yourself comfortable or apprehensive in Nature?

🏹 Do you prefer your condo to camping?

🏹 How powerfully do animal symbols impact your life—mentally, spiritually, and emotionally?

🏹 Do you already work with animal symbols (carvings, imagery, parts) frequently in your magick?

Answering these types of questions should give you a very good feel for whether you're heading in the right direction. If you find yourself apprehensive even thinking about being alone in Nature for more than a few minutes at a time, it's going to be very difficult to develop a relationship with natural spirits. On the other hand, if you find that animal symbols are deeply meaningful to you, and that they provide you with new dimensions to your magick, this is definitely a Path worth your consideration.

Know, too, that even if you find after a time that animal magick wasn't quite the right tact for you, the knowledge and methods won't go to waste. For one thing, what we're presenting here can be adapted and applied to a different focus without too much fuss. For another, your life and connection to Nature will be all the richer for having taken even a brief walk on the wild side.

Chapter 2

The Scientific Dimension: Behavior, Environment, and Habitat

Before you can use a thing, you should strive to understand the function and purpose behind the thing. Ergo, before you rush out to adopt an animal as a totem, or endeavor to work any magick involving an animal species, you should have an idea of where that animal fits into the natural and magickal world. Bears are found all over the planet, but their habitats and behaviors differ. Horses and deer might look similar, but they belong to two distinct categories and their feeding preferences are different. Rather than clutter this chapter with the academic aspects of wildlife biology, refer to Appendix C for a detailed listing of the animal kingdom, as biologists perceive them.

There isn't enough room in this book to go into detail about every animal species (which number more than 1.5 million known), so we will concentrate on the more popular totem species, their natural environments, and their behaviors. Once you get a feel for the "real" animal, then you can start working on how you wish to relate this information to the "totem" animal.

We can't stress the importance of this distinction enough! As a case in point, one of the festivals Rowan attended felt the need to make note in their village guidebook that Gathering participants SHOULD NOT approach the local raccoons, no matter how friendly they might seem or how much of a totem-connection might be perceived!

Aside from carrying rabies and distemper, raccoons have the well-deserved reputation of being able to turn around in their skins and deliver an incredibly vicious bite. And just because it is a wild animal baby does not mean you will be safe from fangs or claws, either. Rowan operated a Georgia State licensed wildlife rehabilitation center for two years and has continued to assist other rehabilitators since then. She has been attacked, chewed, bitten, and clawed by many adorable little creatures doing what comes naturally to wild animals.

So what do animal behaviors in the wild have to do with connecting with a totem spirit? Everything! Most people perceive otters as playful, and they are; but they are also nippy, and simple play can become very aggressive very quickly! Can you handle that kind of energy if you should choose to invoke Otter? Bears are considered the model of maternal protection instinct, but bears are also unpredictable. Even animal behaviorists who study bears cannot say for certain what will cause a bear to attack or how to avoid such an encounter. Invoke Bear energy with caution, unless you want those around you to be constantly on edge! When you invoke the essence or spirit of an animal, you are invoking the entire animal, and it behooves you to understand what it is that you are invoking.

In the classes and orders that follow, please keep in mind that it's our intention to focus mainly on the science of animals in this chapter. This creates a strong foundation on which to build your understanding of Nature's intricacies. In turn, such foundations also improve the results achieved in animal magick simply because your comprehension of, and appreciation for, all the energies represented is far more complete. With this in mind, as you read the remainder of this chapter stop periodically and ask yourself questions such as:

- ✱ How might this animal's habitat affect its spiritual energy for animal magick? For example, a creature that swims is more likely to carry that water energy in the astral realm, too.

- ✱ What are this animal's natural aptitudes, demeanors, and characteristics, and how might those affect my magick for boon or bane?

- ✱ How does this creature interact with other creatures? Who is predator and who is prey? (This will affect your ritual work.)

- ✱ How might this animal's physical structure and natural behaviors influence its symbolic value in spellcraft and other magickal processes?

You can compare the ideas and answers you come up with to the materials presented in the remainder of the book for even more options.

The discussion of the animal kingdom will start with those species humans most easily identify as "animals." The descriptions in the first four classes will only be a quick synopsis of the animals found in each class because there tends to be more similarities than differences in the types of physiology and habitat among these species. The orders following the classes will go into much more detail regarding the individual members of each order.

The Fishes:
Classes Myxini, Cephalaspidomorphi, Chondrichthyes, and Osteichthyes

Welcome to the doorway of the phylum Chordata! Members of this phylum have one integral thing in common: they all have notochords—a flexible rod-like structure that provides dorsal support, and carries the central nervous system the length of the body. From fishes to mammals, whether made of cartilage or bone, simple or complex, all members of this phylum have a spine.

Fish start our survey and study of the animal kingdom because, for most people, the other living creatures that inhabit our earth are so different from us (for example, unicellular animals) that it can be hard for us to feel any type of connection with them.

All fish are aquatic. Evolutionary adaptations include (but are not limited to) fins, gills, mucus-covered skin, protective scales, air bladders for floatation, lateral lines for increased water current and vibration sensitivity, external chemo-receptors for "smelling," as well as excellent olfactory and visual senses. Some are further adapted for living in a salt-water environment, and a few can move between salt and fresh water habitats without serious physiological damage.

The fish class is divided into two superclasses: Agnatha (meaning "jawless") and Gnathostomata (meaning "jawed"). Superclass Agnatha is further broken down into classes Myxini (the hagfishes) and Cephalaspidomorphi (the lampreys).

Superclass Gnathostomata includes the class Chondrichthyes (cartilaginous fishes) with subclass Elasmobranchii (sharks, skates, rays) and subclass Holocephali (chimaeras/ghostfish). Superclass Gnathostomata also includes class Osteichthyes (bony fish), with subclass Crossopterygii (lobe-finned fishes), subclass Dipneusti (lungfishes), and subclass Actinopterygii (ray-finned fishes).

The Amphibians: Class Amphibia

There are more than 3,900 species of amphibians that are divided into three extant (living) orders: the salamanders (Caudata); the toads and frogs (Anura), and the tropical earthworm-like caecilians (Gymnophiona).

Like reptiles and fish, amphibians are ectothermic, meaning they cannot self-regulate their body temperatures, but instead must rely on their environment for body heating and cooling. Animals that can metabolize consumed calories into internal heat energy, such as birds and mammals, are endothermic.

Amphibians represent the evolutionary bridge between strictly aquatic species and strictly terrestrial species, hence their scientific class name, Amphibia, which is Greek for "both/double" (*amphi*), and "life" (*bios*). It was in this class that air-breathing lungs were developed, and the ability to walk on land was first seen. Even today, the majority of amphibians begin life in an aquatic environment, with gills and fins. Adulthood is characterized by the appearance of legs, lungs, and eyelids. Nonetheless, amphibians do not have the freedom to roam far from wet or moist habitats because their skin is thin and subject to desiccation (drying). In fact, while all amphibians can absorb oxygen through their skin to facilitate respiration, some salamanders depend entirely on their skin for breathing. These salamanders have neither gills, nor lungs! The family Plethodontidae, which includes most of the familiar North American species of salamanders, is a good example.

The Reptiles: Class Reptilia

Reptiles were the first truly terrestrial vertebrates, ruling this planet for 160 million years during the Jurassic and Cretaceous periods of the Mesozoic era. There are 7,000 remaining species in this class, of which approximately 300 species are found in North America; however, there are no reptiles in Rowan's home state of Alaska!

Reptiles are divided into four groups: 1) lizards and snakes, 2) crocodilians, 3) turtles, and 4) the tuataras of New Zealand, a sole surviving relic stock.

There are two important adaptations that distinguish reptiles from amphibians. Reptiles have a dry, scaly, almost glandless skin that resists desiccation, and they can lay their eggs on land because a hard shell protects their eggs. Reptiles are also capable of internal fertilization, and their pulmonary and circulatory systems are much more developed than those of the amphibians.

The Birds: Class Aves

There are 8,600 species of birds worldwide: they represent the second largest group of vertebrates. The most unique feature of birds is their feathers, a feature that first appeared approximately 150 million years ago with a creature known as *Archeopteryx*. Other characteristics of the class Aves includes forelimbs that have evolved into wings; hindlimbs adapted for walking, swimming, or perching; horny beaks; hollow bones; and the ability to lay eggs.

Birds are most closely related to reptiles, and their egg-laying ability is one of their connections. Their scaled feet are another, and if you look at their feathers under a microscope, you'll see that a feather is made up of tiny overlapping scales as well.

The Aquatic Sea Mammals: Order of Pinnipedia, Cetacea, and Sirenia

Probably one of the most remarkable things about the aquatic sea mammal orders is the number of families associated with each order, and the number of genus within each family. All members of these orders are adapted to saltwater; however, some are also found in freshwater. All had front legs that have evolved into flippers, and most feed predominately on fish, crustaceans, bivalves, squid, and/or plankton, though some are strictly herbaceous. Some, such as the Cetaceans and the Sirens, lack hindlimbs, but have instead developed tail flukes for locomotion. Another adaptation, found only in the whale and dolphin species, is a breathing hole, located on the top of the head, which allows these animals to intake air while moving rapidly through the water.

The majority of the animals in these orders are social and some, such as the Cetacea, are considered to be highly intelligent, possessing complex forms of communication, primarily as intricate clicks and whistles. The Cetaceans are especially remarkable in that some species have evolved echolocation techniques to assist with navigation and hunting. Animals that utilize echolocation emit a stream of loud, low-frequency clicks. When this stream encounters an object, the sound is bounced back to the creature and processed in the brain as a three dimensional picture, complete with distance information. The only terrestrial (land) species that we know of that possesses this ability is the bat.

Migration behavior is also common among the sea mammals. Many species of whales are known to travel hundreds and sometimes thousands of miles between summer and winter feeding waters. Harp seals (*Phoca groenlandica*) migrate up to 1,000 miles each way each year from Greenland to Newfoundland. Most dolphin species stay within their territorial waters, though the bottle-nosed dolphin (*Tursiops truncatus*) is considered to be migratory, with an Atlantic coast range from New Brunswick to Mexico. The slow-moving manatee will migrate, but their range is restricted to warm tropical and subtropical waters.

The Seal Family:
Otariidae, Phocidae, Monachinae, and Odobenidae

The order Pinnipedia includes the eared seals (family Otariidae), the hair seals (families Phocidae and Monachinae), and the walruses (family Odobenidae). All told, there are 34 species worldwide in this order.

The eared seals have small external ears and hind flippers that can be rotated forward to assist with movement on land. Sea lions and northern fur seals are in this genus.

The hair seals, also known as "true" seals, are ear-less, with hind flippers set behind the tail and incapable of forward rotation, forcing these animals to rely primarily on their powerful front quarters for terrestrial navigation. Common species include the harbor seal, bearded seal, harp seal, ringed seal, gray seal, hooded seal, and northern elephant seal.

The walruses are like a combination of the two seal families. On one hand, they have rotating hind flippers, like the eared seals; on the other hand, they do not have external ears, like the hair seals. Uniquely, they have very little hair on their bodies, and both sexes possess large ivory tusks.

Most species in these families prefer the colder waters of the Arctic, and northern Pacific and Atlantic Oceans; however, some species will commonly travel as far south as the Gulf of California on the west coast, and North Carolina on the east coast. Members of the order Pinnipedia are well-suited to frigid seas. Thick layers of fat (blubber) under hides of dense fur insulate seals from water temperatures that would kill a human in a matter of minutes. While the poor walrus lacks a fur coat, his thick hide and insulating blubber protects him from harm.

Members of the order Pinnipedia are colony animals, meaning that they socially congregate in breeding and feeding locations. One of the few exceptions to this colony behavior is the arctic circumpolar bearded seal (*Erignathus barbatus*), which is not only considered nongregarious, but also nonmigratory. As already mentioned, some species migrate great distances, though the seal that travels the farthest north in the northern hemisphere is the ringed seal (*Phoca hispida*), normally living along the circumpolar Arctic coasts, but found even at the North Pole.

During mating season, the male Pinnipedia species generally form "harems," with one male sexually servicing as many females as he can manage to protect from the other males. As is common in most animal species, male seals and walruses become increasingly aggressive as the breeding season nears, and fighting is frequent and often brutal, though rarely fatal. The females take no part in the mate-selection process; in fact, a male may attack a female of his harem should she attempt to join a neighboring harem.

Females usually give birth to only one pup a year (there is some variation between species). The males take no part in the rearing process, nor do they contribute to the feeding needs of the females while they are nursing their pups. As a result, some species utilize "nursery" areas where the pups gather while their mothers are off hunting. Research has shown that in these circumstances, each mother and pup recognize each other's "voice," allowing the female to locate her pup among the hundreds that might be congregated together. Adoption of orphaned pups by other nursing females is rare: should the mother die, her pup is often doomed to starve. As horrible as this may seem, it bears remembering that life is an interconnecting web: one individual's misfortune is often another individual's good fortune. There are other creatures that rely on the seals for *their* survival—nothing goes to waste in Nature.

The Whale Family: Ziphiidae, Physeteridae, Kogiidae, Monodontidae, Delphinidae, Eschrichtiidae, Balaenopteridae, and Balaenidae

This order of 76 species is divided into two suborders, the toothed whales (dolphins, porpoises, and sperm whales) and the baleen whales (rorquals, right whales, and gray whales). All species have anterior limbs modified into broad flippers, hind limbs that are completely absent, a tail that is split into transverse fleshy flukes, and some species have dorsal fins. In addition, they generally do not possess hair, skin glands, or external ears. They all have lungs, breathing air through a single or double blowhole (nostrils) on the top of the head. All female cetaceans give birth to live young (as opposed to eggs), and possess mammary glands.

You might find it interesting that the largest mammal, the baleen-bearing blue whale, manages to reach its extraordinary size of up to 106 feet in length and 104 tons in weight on a diet of filtered plankton and krill! As a matter of fact, the blue whale is believed to be the largest animal ever to have existed, considered to be two to three times larger than the greatest Mesozoic dinosaur, *Brontosaurus*.

There is something about the Cetaceans that evokes a sense of awe in humans. There is a grace, a simplicity, and an elegance about these animals that makes us want to interact with them. Of course, it's important not to confuse fantasy with reality— all cetaceans are potentially dangerous to humans, whether they possess teeth or baleen. Yet despite the dangers, humans are driven by some inexplicable need to get closer to these seemingly gentle giants, and there are reports and legends that support the belief that some cetaceans feel driven to interact with humans as well. Maritime stories are full of accounts of dolphins and porpoises coming to the aid of near-drowning sailors. Some fishermen believe that killer whales (orcas) lead them to schools of harvestable fish. Rowan has seen a humpback whale stop an 85-foot tour boat because it insisted on conducting its own sightseeing excursion by swimming 30 feet off the side of the boat (much to the delight of the boat passengers). And then there was a pod of dall porpoises that she once saw swim to a boat from a distance of more than a half mile away so they could then frolic around the boat for a full 20 minutes! Of course, it makes it very hard for a boat captain to be in compliance with the Marine Mammal Protection Act, which requires all boats in Alaskan and Hawaiian waters to maintain a distance of 100 yards from humpback whales, and forbids acts of "harassment" toward other marine mammals nationwide, when the animals themselves refuse to abide by the law. Nonetheless, the laws are designed to protect these creatures, and while we may not be able to (or even want to) discourage a curious whale or dolphin, we can be responsible for our own actions.

The Manatee Family: Trichechidae

There are four extant species in this order: the Dugong ("sea cow") species of the tropical coastlines of east Africa, Asia, and Australia, and the three species of manatees of the Caribbean area, Amazon River, and west Africa. A fifth species, the Stellar sea cow, was hunted to extinction in the mid-18th century.

As improbable as it may seem, manatees are likely the original source of the mermaid myths, though how anyone could imagine the rather homely manatee as a lovely, seductive sea nymph remains a mystery. Too many lonely male sailors, too many months at sea, and perhaps a bit too much grog!

The manatees are characterized by a large head, six instead of the standard seven cervical vertebra, no hindlimbs, forelimbs modified as flippers, and ranging between 10 and 13 feet in length. They are strictly vegetarians, slowly grazing their way through both fresh and salt waters. Interestingly, manatees are distantly related to elephants.

While generally solitary animals, manatees will congregate in prime feeding areas. Sadly, these beautifully ugly creatures are frequent victims of careless human boating activities. Almost all manatees occupying the navigable waterways in the southern United States bear scars from encounters with boat propellers. They, like so many of the sea mammals, are also helpless victims of well-meaning humans who selfishly want to interact with these slow-moving aquatic herbivores.

All marine mammals are protected by Federal law: it is illegal to commit any act that may be construed as "harassment," such as attempting to come into close contact with these animals, for the presence of a human in an animal's natural habitat is often perceived as a threat. So, while it may be very tempting to swim with the wild manatees, please restrain these self-centered desires and learn how to simply enjoy these animals from a distance.

The Flesh-eating Mammals: Order Carnivora

There are 240 of some of the strongest and most intelligent predatory species that belong to the order Carnivora. Mammalian carnivores (meat-eaters) are located all over the world, except in Australia and the Antarctic where there are no indigenous species that belong to this order. Members of this order have specialized teeth, known as carnassial teeth, which are designed specifically to tear flesh. All of a carnivore's teeth are sharp-edged, even the molars, in direct contrast to the flat, grinding teeth found in herbivores. Physiologically speaking, members of the order Carnivora are very similar to humans. Like humans, carnivores have eyes located more forward in the skull to allow for depth perception: a necessary adaptation for hunting. They also tend to have large brains, which means they have a capacity for intelligence. Unlike humans, carnivores generally have mobile ears placed high upon the head for increased hearing and long sinus cavities that allow them to distinguish a greater range of odors. Perhaps it is because of our similarities to the carnivore species that we humans have such a love-hate relationship with them.

The Dog Family: Canidae

Commonly referred to as "man's best friend," the loyal dog is a member of the family Canidae, along with the wolves, coyotes, jackals, foxes, and wild dog species (such as dingos). While all of these species share common characteristics, it's interesting to note that only the fox has pupils that will contract in bright daylight to mere slits (similar to a cat's). I should also mention that the dingo was the only nonmarsupial animal on the continent of Australia when it was discovered by Europeans, though the dingo is not native to Australia and its origin is unknown.

All of the canine species tend to be social animals, though not all of them live in packs, which are generally extended family units. Those that *do* live in packs adhere to a strict hierarchy system. There is only one alpha male and alpha female. Normally this pair mates for life and usually they are the only ones to mate within the pack. An evolutionary advantage is the adaptability of the canine species. Wild canines are frequently found in proximity to humans, quite willing to substitute domestic livestock as a preferred food for wild game. This willingness to compromise on the part of the wild canines does not, of course, make them very popular with farmers or ranchers, but one must admire their ability to survive despite the pressures they face from us. In nature, wild canines play an important predator role. They maintain prey species' populations and overall health by culling the sick, aged, and weak from the environment. Perhaps this is the real reason why humans tend to fear the wolf (and other predators) so much: not because they offer us competition for food and space, but because we fear that we may be the ones "culled" should we attempt to coexist with this and other spectacular predator(s). Interestingly, recorded cases of nonrabid, unprovoked wolf attacks on humans are extremely rare, especially in North America. Even in the rare cases where a wolf has attacked a human, there were extenuating circumstances: depletion of local game species leading to starvation conditions in the wolf packs; situations where domestic dogs were involved, so that the wolf may have actually been after the dog but the human got in the way; conditions where the wolf may have become habituated to humans (such as at campgrounds); or cases where the human (usually a child) ran from a wolf, eliciting an instinctual chase-behavior. Yet humans walk a fine line between being classified as a prey species and a predator species, and so our fears remain. On the other hand, there are many cases of attacks on humans by feral dogs, and the dog-like hyena is a particular menace to humans in Africa, so maybe not all of our fears are unfounded.

Of the wild canine species, wolves are Rowan's favorite, and she often makes parallels between wolf behavior and human behavior. Reproductively speaking, both species (wolves and human) tend to form lasting pair-bonds. Both species will, however, take another mate if the first dies. The females of both species, while capable of mating at a young age (as young as 10 months for a wolf, 12 years for the average human), normally do not reproduce until much older (late teens, early 20s for both species—bearing in mind that one human year is equivalent to five canine years). In fact, wolves do not fully mature, hormonally, until they are about 5 years old (or 25 human years of age). While humans do not have an estrus cycle, per se, both wolves and humans tend to become pregnant only once a year. Wolves because they only come into estrus once a year, and humans because the length of pregnancy is nine months long.

There are social similarities as well. Both species tend to prefer extended family units, as opposed to living alone, or with nonrelated members of the same species. Wolves and humans require strong leadership to maintain social bonds, and both establish systems of hierarchy to promote order. Both are territorial, and will fight to protect territorial rights. And finally, both display altruistic behavior: caring for orphaned young; providing for aged or injured members of the social group; and defending the home and members of the society from outside threats.

The domestic dog was originally bred from these wild canines, and they possess many of their wild brethren's attributes. In fact, humans have selectively bred domestic canine species to emphasis some wild characteristics such as sociability (pack behavior), herding and sporting (hunting behavior), and protectiveness (territorial behavior). No one really knows when man first attempted to domesticate wild canines, but it is reasonable to assume that humans and canines have had a long and mutually beneficial relationship.

The Bear Family: Ursidae

Bears are awe-inspiring creatures, the largest of the living terrestrial carnivores. Their size, strength, and nature have caused them to be revered and feared by humans since the dawn of time. Bears belong to the family Ursidae. There are three bear species in North America: the black bear (*Ursus americanus*); the grizzly, or brown, bear (*Ursus arctos horribilis* and *Ursus arctos middendorffi*), and the polar bear (*Ursus maritimus*). Of the three, the brown bear of coastal Alaska (commonly referred to as a Kodiak bear) is the largest, reaching a height of up to 10 feet and a weight of more than 1,200 pounds.

For years the "panda bear" (*Ailuropoda melanoleuca*) was not consider a member of the bear family at all, but rather a member of the raccoon family, Procyonidae. However, according to the *2000 International Union for Conservation of Nature and Natural Resources (IUCN) Red List of Threatened Species*, the panda is currently being listed as a member of the family Ursidae (bear).

Unlike the canine family, bears are not considered to be social animals. Though exceptions have been documented, cubs generally stay with their mother for about two years, after which the sow (female bear) will run them off in preparation for her next litter of cubs. Females usually give birth during the winter to one or two cubs, litters larger than two are rare. Adult male bears are often considered a lethal threat to cubs, and females with young are notorious for their aggressive protectiveness due to this fact. Sadly, many people have been attacked because of this instinctual behavior. But bears are not always easy to judge, they can be very unpredictable. A bear that allows one person to come close for a photograph will run a mile just to attack another person who happens to be passing through its territory. Some bears become habituated to humans to the point of extreme tolerance; others will become totally intolerant because of habituation. The bottom line is that bears are dangerous and should be treated, both in flesh and spirit form, with respect.

All bears are territorial, demarcating their boundaries with claw scratches and scent-markings. While bears will not tolerate company when feeding on a freshly-killed carcass, most bears will accept the presence of other bears (and other animals, including humans) when engaged in seasonal feeding activities such as post-hibernation grazing, berry harvesting, and fishing during the spawn. All bears are omnivores, meaning they will eat insect, animal, and plant material, but depending on the species and environment, some bears tend to consume more of one than the other. Bears in the colder regions of North America will hibernate during the winter months. This can be a full hibernation, where the bear retreats to a den and stays in a deep sleep-state for several months, or a partial-hibernation where the bear will retreat to the den only during extremely cold temperatures, but will emerge to feed during warm periods. This ability to hibernate has long fascinated scientists, for a hibernating animal does not eat or eliminate waste material and is capable of greatly reducing their cardiac and respiratory functions. A better understanding of this phenomenon would have great impact on the fields of medicine and astronautics.

The Cat Family: Felidae

From house kitties to cougars, cats are members of the family Felidae. There are several adaptations that set cats apart from other carnivore species. First, cats have retractable claws, which they continuously sharpen. Second, their clavicles (collarbones) do not articulate with their scapulae (shoulder blade) or sternums. Third, their tongues are unusually rough, due to sharp, horny, backward-directed papillae. And finally, most (but not all) of the cats have pupils that contract into vertical slits when exposed to bright light.

The largest of the North American cats is the jaguar, ranging 6 to 8 feet in length, and weighing up to 250 pounds. The largest of the entire cat family is the tiger. There are two species of tigers, the Siberian, which can measure up to 13 feet in length and weigh around 700 pounds, and the Bengal, which averages 10 feet long and up to 500 pounds. Both species are found only in Asia.

By and large, cats are solitary creatures. Even people who have cats are aware that their pet only associates with them when it's convenient for the cat. The ancient Egyptians worshipped the cat—and little wonder—cats possess in innate regalness. Maybe it's their independence. Perhaps it's the way that they move. Or it could be the way that they can focus all of their attention on one tiny detail, effectively blocking out whatever chaos surrounds them. Whatever the reason, humans react to cats in a definite bipolar fashion: we either love them, or we hate them, but we are rarely indifferent to them.

The Hoofed Mammals: Order of Perissodactyla and Artiodactyla

Hoofed animals are divided into two categories: those with an even number of toes, and those with an odd number. Hooves are nothing more than fused toes with an extra-big fingernail. These categories are further broken down into two more groups: those who are ruminants and those who aren't.

Ruminants are Ungulates (hoofed mammals) that possess four stomachs (the rumen, reticulum, omasum, and abomasum). Ruminants do not automatically digest their food once it is ingested. They stuff their rumens during their feeding periods, then retire someplace quiet to hack it back up and chew the cud. It's the masticated mass that gets digested. As a rule, ruminants do not possess canine teeth (although there are deer that have vestigial canine teeth), and often do not have upper incisor teeth either; an upper cartilaginous pad is present instead. By the way, deer with canine teeth are really wicked looking! Like a vampire version of Bambi. Take *that* image with you into trance!

The other group of Ungulates has only one stomach and does not chew cud. They also are more likely to have upper incisors, though the canine teeth are still lacking. Horses and rhinoceroses are in this group.

All Ungulates are herbivores (plant-eaters). Some, such as deer and goats, tend to be browsers, meaning that they feed predominately off of leaves, twigs, and high grasses. Others, such as horses, sheep, and cattle are grazers and they feed on ground-level vegetation. Of the two feeding styles, grazers tend to be more damaging to the environment because they remove plant life that secures soil.

Now, having made all of the above definitive statements regarding Ungulates, I have to backpedal a bit in order to discuss pigs. Pigs are Ungulates. The similarity ends there. Pigs are omnivores. They don't so much graze or browse as they do wander around eating anything they can root up. They have both incisors and canine teeth; the latter commonly referred to as tusks. Their stomachs are more complex than a simple stomach, but not quite as complicated as a ruminant stomach. Of all the Ungulate species, the pig family is the most hazardous to an ecosystem, for they are capable of absolutely destroying plant life and degrading water systems.

One final note on Ungulates: Some Ungulates have horns, some have antlers, and some have neither. Horns and antlers are not the same thing. Horns are comprised of a bony core covered by a sheath of keratinous material (the same material that makes up hair and nails). Horns continue to grow during the entire life of the animal. Horns are not shed. On the other hand, antlers are shed yearly. Antlers are hard structures that start off as living bone, covered in a blood-rich material called "velvet" and then ossify into dead bone. Antlers are sensitive to damage when still covered in velvet and some really weird looking racks have been observed as a result of injury sustained while still in velvet.

For those of you who like to hunt, let me mention that three factors determine antler growth: *age*, *genetics*, and *diet*. The best genetics in the world won't produce a big antlered rack in a starving deer, regardless of age; nor will an old buck with plenty of food grow a huge set of antlers if his genetic material is poor. So it is possible for a 3-year-old buck with good genetics and diet to have a rack that is larger than a 5-year-old buck. Just thought I'd set that straight for the record.

The Deer Family: Cervidae

So, you're interested in a member of the deer family as a totem? Well, here's what you need to know. They are members of the order Artiodactyla, family Cervidae. All members of this order have even-numbered toes, and include deer, cattle, sheep, goats, pigs, and related animals. The largest member of the deer family is the moose, followed by the elk species. The smallest member is the Chilean pudu, and in North America it is the Key deer. Deer are seasonal social animals. Unlike horses and pigs, which are herd animals, deer tend to form in loose age-related groups of two or three same-sex individuals. Hence, young bucks tend to leave their mothers to hang out with the boys, while the young does tend to stay at home with mom. This pattern changes during breeding season, or the "rut." Breeding does will travel in herds, while breeding bucks are more solitary. Young bucks continue to associate with each other, using the time spent together to hone fighting techniques, while actively trying to avoid the more aggressive, mature bucks.

Deer have the appearance of being sweet, gentle animals. Appearances can be deceiving. Bucks are dangerous during the rut. They have been known to attack people who get too close. Does, while lacking antlers, are not to be underestimated either. The hooves of a deer are very sharp and capable of ripping flesh. Actually, of the two defenses a deer has—antlers and hooves—it's the hooves with which you need to be concerned!

Deer species can be found living all over the world and in many types of habitats. Moose tend to prefer aquatic vegetation, so they congregate in the lake regions. Caribou (reindeer) feed off of lichen and grasses and are capable of surviving in very harsh environments. Elk and deer are usually found in woodlands where they forage for tender leaves, mushrooms, and protein-rich mast (the nuts of trees, such as beech and oak).

The Horse Family: Equidae

Has the horse taken your fancy? Horses are members of the order Perissodactyla, family Equidae. Members of this order have odd-numbered toes and include horses, asses, zebras, tapirs, and rhinoceroses. Horses come in a wide variety of sizes and colors—from the large draft breeds to the relatively new miniature breeds. They are social animals, traveling in herds that are led and protected by the breeding stallion and maintained by a dominant mare. Horses do not form lasting mating bonds; one stallion services all of the mares in the herd.

Fighting can be brutal between stallions and ends only when the loser leaves the herd. Overtly hostile acts among other members of the herd are not common, but when skirmishes do occur, some well-placed kicks and bites reestablish the proper hierarchy. At the risk of anthropomorphizing (assigning human characteristics to nonhuman species), it would appear that some individuals within a herd develop friendships. These equine friends will often feed together, sleep together, and reinforce bonds through mutual grooming behavior.

When threatened, it is the stallion that normally comes to the defense, while the rest of the herd moves quickly to safety. An angry horse is not an animal to challenge! Flailing hooves can crush an attacker's skull or back; wicked bites can tear chunks out of fat and underlying muscle. Because of a horse's strength and speed, the species has few natural predators. Probably the greatest strategical lesson that Horse can teach is to fight only until there is a clear opportunity to flee. This is not cowardly—this is survival.

The Pig Family: Suina

Pigs are more nobly referred to as "boars." Actually, "boar" is the term normally reserved for the male of the pig species (a female is called a "sow"), or for either sex of the nondomesticated, wild species, but for some reason you just never seem to hear someone claim that they have a "pig" or "sow" totem. Maybe it's because the word "pig" has such negative connotations in our society: "You act like a pig" (gluttonous); "You smell like a pig" (unwashed); "You are a pig" (a slop)—the list goes on and on. The irony is that pigs are intelligent, courageous, clean, and highly adaptable animals.

Pigs (also referred to as "hogs" or "swine") are in the order Artiodactyla, family Suina. This even-toed family includes pigs, peccaries, and hippopotamuses. Pigs are generally social animals, though some species prefer a more solitary life.

Pigs are omnivores. They will eat just about anything, from invertebrates and insects (such as worms and beetles), to small mammals (such as mice, eggs, and chicks), to plants (including, but not limited to, nuts, mushrooms, roots, berries, and herbs). Pigs have an excellent sense of smell, and have been used by humans for years to locate valuable truffles hidden beneath the forest floor.

Wild pigs were first domesticated almost 9,000 years ago in China. Christopher Columbus and the Spanish explorers introduced swine to the Americas. Many of the feral hogs are descended from these animals and others who have escaped farmers in the past.

You do not want to stumble upon a wild or feral pig! Wild pigs are ferocious fighters and will not hesitate to attack if they feel the least bit threatened. They are capable of killing much larger predators, including man, by inflicting painful bites and goring adversaries with their tusks, which are modified upper and lower canine teeth that continue to grow for the life of the animal (similar to the incisor teeth of rodents). Boars came to be associated with courage and valor because of their determination to continue attacking, even when mortally wounded. South American peccary females, in an attempt to protect their piglets, have been known to confront jaguars and win. And woe be to the hunter that gets caught off-guard in the territory of these pigs, for they will run a human right up a tree and then lay siege to the poor human for hours.

It is well known that pigs are highly intelligent, prized as pets and working companions. Contrary to popular belief, pigs are also clean animals, but the lack of sweat glands means that they must have a method to keep cool during hot weather, be it by bathing in mud or water. In the wild, mud has the added advantage of protecting their hides from biting insects, as well as from sunburn.

Domestic pigs are relatively easy to maintain; pigs can be housebroken and trained in much the same fashion as a dog. Those who raise pigs on farms normally keep the animals in a fenced pen, usually turning them loose into harvested fields or surrounding woodlands in the Fall and Winter to forage and fatten up.

In Conclusion

While we realize that the scientific element sometimes feels a bit cumbersome, to the wild Witch it's essential knowledge. If we wish to honor something and work in partnership with it, we have to first look at it critically in the temporal, or physical, world. That's the "below" part of the "as above, so below" maxim. Now that you've taken the time to get a better feel for animal classifications, habitats, and natural behaviors, you can move on to applying that knowledge "above," practically and wisely in your animal magick.

Chapter 3

Bird's Eye View: Animal Omens, Signs, and Divinations

All nature's creatures join to express nature's purpose. Somewhere in their mounting and mating, rutting and butting is the very secret of nature itself.

—Graham Swift

Whether a nation or a family, if it is about to flourish there will be fortunate signs, and when about to perish, there will be evil omens.

—Confucius

Animals figure heavily into divination methods, typically by their symbolic value at the time of observation, or by patterns created during ritual sacrifice. While most modern practitioners will not sacrifice a living creature to foretell the future, there are many other options to consider ranging from interpreting random encounters to watching for animal imagery in dreams. Better still, because our ancestors were diligently observant of their environment, we are slowly discovering that some portents actually have foundations in science.

For example, the old saying goes that when the swallows fly low, rain will soon follow. This bit of lore has been proven very sound. Apparently the swallows are following the insects that are moving away from stormy areas of the atmosphere. Balancing the scientific element, the modern wild Witch might ask, *But what does this mean metaphysically?* Well, based on customary interpretations and meteorological information it could certainly mean one should carry an umbrella. Or more figuratively it might foretell a personal storm on the horizon. This is an excellent illustration of exactly the kind of divination this chapter explores.

Astragalomancy, Scapulimancy, Plastromancy

These giant, nearly unpronounceable words simply mean divination by animal bones and shells. Plastromancy originated in China around 1500 B.C.E. The basic process at that time entailed heating a poker and applying it to a sanctified bone. The cracks on the surface were then interpreted. By 100 B.C.E. specific instructions in this art appeared for use in the Chinese imperial court, with the most popular medium for interpretation being a turtle shell (perhaps because of the mythology of the turtle bearing the Universe on its back).

The Japanese had similar methods that appeared in popular use around the 7th century A.D. and continued until the 1800s! They, too, preferred turtle shells, or periodically the shoulder of a deer. Typically, a sect of Shinto priests called the *Jingikan* performed this divinatory rite by fasting for a week previous to the reading and avoiding any contact with blood. Breaking either taboo would hinder the priest's ability to perform the ritual.

As one might expect after taking such great precautions the ritual for the *Jingiken* was similarly painstaking. He used a cherry twig, a knife, and a chisel to carve and shape a symbol in the turtle shell. The cherry twig was heated until red-hot and then placed in the symbol's crevices, first along the singular vertical line, then along the two horizontal ones. When cracks began to appear, wet bamboo sticks were shaken over the shell to enhance the cracking effect. Lastly, ink was poured into the cracks to make the pattern even more pronounced, and the shell was interpreted. Generally speaking, cracks upward and to the right held positive meanings, and those downward or to the left were negative.

I should mention at this juncture that the people of the Far East were certainly not alone in these types of practices. Celts had similar procedures using hot coals and the shoulder bone of a pig, as did Romans using sheep bones. The Greeks cast lots using knucklebones from sheep, while both the Zulu tribes and Bantu used a variety of animal bones for various types of divinatory castings.

South African Shamans utilized bones and shells, along with various other media for their divinations. Any inquiries took place during the new moon, and it seems as if the interpretive values for each item were left to oral histories. The Shaman used abalone shell for financial questions, cowrie shells in decision-making, and spiral shells to determine the best timing for any event, in combination with the bones from chickens, which had different meanings depending on how they landed in a casting.

Because it's highly unlikely that anyone reading this book will pursue these more arcane methods, let's move on to considering other forms of animal divination that can easily be applied or adapted to our modern world.

Chance Meetings and Sightings

You're walking down a pathway, minding your own business, and a rabbit suddenly crosses in front of you. Now, if this happened in a park-like setting, you might think nothing of it. Hey, it's only a "bunny," right? That's not what our ancestors thought. Random encounters with Nature's citizens were written up as having specific meaning, and people trusted these omens.

In particular, bird augury (ornithomancy) was among the most trusted of chance signs and omens. The Hittites catalogued more than 27 species of birds and the meaning of their movements by 1330 B.C.E. Greeks felt eagles, crows, and vultures were typically messengers, while the Celts preferred crows, eagles, and wrens. Tibetans observed crows, taking note of the time, direction, and intensity of this bird's cry (a caw heard form the west was the best sign, while from the southwest it implied a forthcoming profit).

Here are more bird signs:

Bird (egg): Finding a whole one is very good luck. You will avoid trouble! Wrap this carefully in a white cloth (the color of protection) and carry it as an amulet or put it in a safe place at home to keep your sacred space free of aggravation.

Bird (red): A wish coming true, especially when flying upward or toward the east.

Bluebird: Happiness.

Cock: Visitors will soon cross your threshold, so make some magickal munchies!

Crickets: Entering your home brings domestic bliss and friendship.

Crow (cawing): From the southeast: beware of an enemy. This is a good time to do some general protective spells.

Crow (flying): Forthcoming travel, so get those suitcases out of storage and make a safe travel charm with a piece of turquoise to accompany you.

Cuckoo: When sited to your right in Spring, a good Summer will follow. Make ritual plans now!

Dove: Peace and joy.

Duck: Stability in a relationship.

Eagle: Success through positive application of personal abilities, so be tenatious.

Gull: Forthcoming travel by sea (or these days, perhaps by air).

Hawk: When one flies over your head, victory or success in a contest is on the horizon.

Hummingbird: Fidelity and fertility.

Owl: Hooting three times precedes a death (literal or figurative).

Raven: Met before battle (of any kind: legal, personal, etc.) implies victory.

Robin: One nesting near your home implies improved luck, where as seeing one first thing in the morning means that you should be on the lookout for guests.

Sparrow: Peace in one's home unless it nests on your window, then it's trouble for lovers. Talk it out.

Woodpecker: Your current efforts will be successful.

Wren: Your prospects are improving.

Let's put some of this information into a few examples that are more concrete. Say you've been out job hunting and getting more and more discouraged. All of a sudden you notice a wren perched outside the place where you just applied. This means job prospects are improving, perhaps at that exact location! Or if you've been waiting for a raise or promotion at the office as part of a review process, and a praying mantis lands on you on the way to work that morning, I'd say your wish is about to come true!

By the way, if you happen to stumble across the feather from a bird, that's an omen, too. Here's a few of the values Greeks gave for the feather's color:

Black:	Literal or figurative death. Bad luck.
Black and white:	Averting trouble.
Blue:	Love and joy.
Blue, white, and black:	New love, relationship(s), or partnerships.
Brown:	Good health (or health improvements).
Brown and white:	Happiness.
Gray:	Peace.
Gray and white:	A wish fulfilled.
Green:	An adventure.
Green and black:	Fame and fortune.
Orange:	Delight.
Purple:	An exciting trip.
Red:	Good luck.
Yellow:	False friends or companions, so be careful.

Rinse the feather carefully, pat it dry, then keep it somewhere safe. These make great components for spells, charms, amulets, talismans, power pouches, etc. For example, after finding the blue feather, you decide you want to strengthen a friendship. You might put that feather in a power pouch for your friend as a token of love and the joy you hope they experience. Or if you find difficulties on the horizon after finding the black and white feather, perhaps you could burn the feather to banish the troubles.

And what of the rest of the animal kingdom? What did random encounters with other creatures mean? Here's a brief sampling.

Adder: Omen of good luck. Kill the first one you see in the Spring to ensure your triumph over your enemies (to allow it to escape is to court disaster and bad luck). Seen by the front door is an omen of death (old English belief).

Ant: An ant nest near your home is an omen of providence.

Bats: Flying near you means someone is trying to betray or bewitch you. Flying around the house three times, or to actually fly into a room is an indication of death or very bad luck to someone you know.

Bear: Be confident with regard to a personal goal, and pay close attention to your instincts.

Bees: Flying around you they bring news (potentially from Spirit); landing but not stinging, they portend luck especially for those in leadership positions. Bees that swarm on a dead tree or hedge are an omen of death in the family; it is also bad if a stray swarm lands on your house or land. In Wales, a bee flying around a sleeping child means she will have a good life.

Beetle: Walking over your shoe brings luck for the day. A beetle crawling over your shoe can also be an omen of death. Scottish superstition holds that it is bad luck if a beetle enters a room of your home wherein your family is seated, and it's even worse luck to kill the beetle.

Butterfly: Coming into your home means a wedding or partnership. Gently capture the creature and release it with a wish!

Cat (black) crossing road:
The next person passing that spot will have a wish fulfilled.

Cat (calico): Seeing or meeting one brings good luck on a new endeavor.

Cat (stray): Stroke this creature to encourage luck; feed it to encourage providence for yourself and those you love.

Deer: Don't harbor unrealistic expectations toward a person or situation.

Dog (black): In Arab tradition this is a negative omen.

Dog (stray): In Babylon the High Priests took note of the stray's fur color: white representing a long wait, and red symbolizing the need to abandon a project. Gray revealed a forthcoming loss, and yellow warned of devastation.

Donkey: Meeting one represents unanticipated burdens.

Dragonfly: Take care with your communications.

Fox: Nearly everywhere but Wales meeting a fox at the outset of an endeavor is a bad omen (in Wales it's a good sign).

Goat: In Europe, the sign of improved fortune.

Hare: Should you see one first thing in the morning, be careful all day. Consider carrying one of your lucky charms.

Horse: Meeting a horse portends very good news coming your way.

Lamb (lone): A solitary lamb predicts joy, peace, and tranquility. If the creature looks at you, add prosperity to the list.

Ladybug: If she lands on you, ask her nicely and she'll fly in the direction of a future lover or living space. Watch where she flies after this.

Lizard: Disappointment or disillusionment (especially with regard to a specific hope or dream). Consider the practicality of your plans.

Mice: Danger or struggle ahead. Divination by mice is called myomancy.

Mole: Appearing in your lawn, you will soon move to a new residence.

Mouse (white):
In Bohemia, the sign of improvement.

Moth: Flying toward you brings an important letter or phone call on its wings.

Pig: Something will soon cause you worry so shore up your defenses.

Praying mantis:
When one lands on your hand, it speaks of well-deserved honors coming to you.

Snake: Entering the home brings luck (however, if you own one and it leaves, it's bad luck).

Weasel: Seeing one during travel is a bad omen. Near your home, beware of familial discord (perhaps perform a cleansing ritual to rid your space of negativity).

Behavioral Portents

Being a pet owner, Trish often watches her animals in wonder. Why does the lizard sleep during the day sometimes, and other times not? Why does the dog hide under the table before a storm? And why does one of her cats (who rarely shows affection) suddenly want to snuggle? Now, if this modern-minded wild Witch finds such activities mind-boggling, Trish can't imagine that our ancestors were any different. In fact, if anything, they'd watch animal behaviors even more closely, seeking out clues to the world in which they lived.

Let's start our examination with cats. This method (officially called felidomancy) originated in Egypt where cats were revered. Here are just a few behavioral portents for our feline friends:

Washing its face: Visitors are coming.

Washing in the doorway: Clergy is coming over (quick, look busy!).

Walking on your cat's tail: Bad luck will follow (any cat owner knows an angry cat is trouble just waiting to happen).

Abandoning house: Really bad omen (move with the cat!).

Stray entering home: A very good omen; money to follow on this creature's tail.

Entering room right paw first:

     If you've been pondering a question the answer is YES!

Sneezing: Improved luck for everyone in
                             your house (except perhaps the
                             cat!).

Meowing during travel: Be cautious; trouble ahead.

Behavioral omens were certainly not restricted to cats, however. A dog entering your house and immediately laying on the bed means you'll soon have new possessions. Then there's predictions based on a dog's howl (called ololygmancy). Typically, hearing a dog howling is a negative omen or warning. To those entering into a partnership of any type, it is doubly so. If you're about to sign legal documents and this happens, I'd seriously consider waiting or reading the fine print far more carefully.

For those of you with fish tanks, they also answer questions. Watch the tank while thinking of a yes or no question. If the fish move to the right, it's positive. If to the left, negative. If they swim in opposite directions, it speaks of two equally appealing options. If they move in circles, no certain answer is available at the moment.

Alternatively, if you're the proud owner of a crab, place it in a bowl of sand and think of your question. Let the crab skitter around for a while. Then scry the results of the patterns made as you might an inkblot!

Trish believes that the best way to learn from the animals in and around our lives is by creating a journal. Once a week write down what's going on in and around your life and note that information. Next, record what those animals are doing (specifically any behaviors that aren't common to them). After a while certain patterns should appear.

Weather or Not?

It seems our ancestors trusted in the citizens of Nature to act as ongoing weather predictors, and if you think about it, this makes perfect sense. Who better to tell us of fair or foul weather than those creatures whose very lives depend on being aware of the elements? Consequently, several animal omen and sign interpretations come under the category of those that foretell the weather.

Albatross: Flying around a ship heralds stormy weather.

Ants: Small ant hills appearing above the sidewalk cracks foretell a day without a chance of rain.

Ants: Stepping on ants brings rain. Particularly active ants (for example, carrying their eggs away from the nest) is an omen of bad weather.

Ants: When ant hills are high in July, there will be a snowy winter.

Bats: Flying at twilight—good weather that night and often the next day. A bat smacking into a building is a sign of rain. A bat flying earlier than normal means good weather is coming.

Bees: Flying late at night foretells of a sunny day on the morrow.

Butterflies: Appearing in the morning indicate sunshine.

Buzzard: Flying high indicates hot weather for several days.

Cat: When leaping playfully, a gale is coming.

Cat: Sitting with back to hearth, a storm is approaching.

Cat: Washing behind its ear means rain or high humidity is coming.

Caterpillar (wooly):
     The wider the band on its back, the milder the winter.

Chickens: Staying out in the rain means that you should expect rain all day.

Cicada:	After the first time you hear this in Summer, expect the first frost of the year in exactly 90 days.
Cocks:	Crowing all day means rain.
Cows:	Restless cows with tails in the air mean rain.
Crane:	Flying quietly and high indicates fair weather.
Crickets:	Chirping loudly means a nice day.
Crows:	Four crows on a hickory limb portend a long, cold Winter.
Dog:	Eating grass indicates severe weather (often tornados).
Dog:	Shivering or rolling around on the floor means a thunderstorm is coming.
Dolphins:	Gathering around a ship indicates bad sea weather ahead.
Flies:	Biting is a rain sign.
Fur:	If the fur on a creature grows thicker than normal, it portends a cold Winter.
Hens:	Cackling is a rain sign (as is hissing geese).
Hogs:	Carrying sticks in their mouth means the weather is changing.
Horse:	Running fast means a storm or winds are approaching.
Robins:	Singing on a barn means good weather.
Rooster:	Crowing in the middle of the night means a really nasty storm is coming (may be a figurative "storm").
Seagull:	When they're on the sand, it's bad boating weather.

Sharks: Going out to sea indicates cold weather moving inland.

Snake: Hunting for food indicates rain.

Spider: Spinning in the rain means it's about to clear.

Squirrel: More nut gathering and thicker tails indicate a harsh Winter.

Swallow: Flying high portends drought.

Woodpecker: Crying indicates wet weather.

If Ducks or Drakes their Wings do flutter high
Or tender Colts upon their Backs do lie,
If Sheep do bleat, or play, or skip about,
Or Swine hide Straw by bearing on their Snout,
If Oxen lick themselves against the Hair,
Or grazing Kine to feed apace appear,
If Cattle bellow, grazine from below,
Or if Dogs Entrails rumble to and fro,
If Doves or Pigeons in the Evening come
Later than usual to their Dove-House Home,
If Crows and Daws do oft themselves be-wet,
Or Ants and Pismires Home a-pace do get,
If in the dust Hens do their Pinions shake,
Or by their flocking a great Number make,
If Swallows fly upon the Water low,
Or Wood-Lice seem in Armies for to go,
If Flies or Gnats, or Fleas infest and bite,
Or sting more than they're wont by Day or Night,
If Toads hie Home, or Frogs do croak amain,
Or Peacocks cry.

—European rhyme (author unknown)

Incidentally, the aforementioned animal behavior diary you've been encouraged to create helps here, too. Begin watching to see how animals behave when it's clear and blue outside versus just prior to and during a rainstorm. Watch to see how they eat in the Fall and Winter. As before, patterns will begin to appear that reflect your locality and on what animal omens and signs you can depend.

As for figuratively interpreting weather omens, just be a little creative. For example, a "warm" weather sign could imply a similar warmth from friends and loved ones. A frosty spell indicates a distancing or emotional coldness; rain might symbolize tears or trials; sunshine represents blessings; drought, a physical or emotional thirst you can't fill; and storms forewarn of stormy situations or relationships.

Creature of My Dreams

The history of dream interpretation reaches far back into the pages of time. While not quite as old as haruspicy, we find written documents dating 1350 B.C.E. in Babylon that speak of various symbols in our dreamscape. In this region it was common to review the whole of a dream for meaning rather than specific parts. Assyrians took just the opposite approach, and reviewed each element as a key to understanding our nightly visitors.

Egyptians had dream oracles. Hittite prayers ask for the gods to reveal themselves in dreams, and they even had a special god who presided over the dream world: Ziqiqu. Hebrews trusted in dreams to indicate the will of YHWH, and Native Americans look to dreams and visionary states as a means of speaking to the spirit world.

Some of the world's most notable minds respected the art of dream divination. Socrates rewrote *Aesop's Fables* because he believed that one of his dreams instructed this course of action. Hippocrates (the father of medicine) felt that dreams could reveal the source of illness, or alternatively symbolize a previously unknown physical problem. Other dream advocates include Julius Caesar, St. John, Mozart, and Benjamin Franklin.

The modern science of psychology, however, is to thank for the ongoing interest in, and popularity of, dream interpretation. Carl Jung's writings at the turn of the century strengthened the foundation of this art, if only as a way that our minds can filter and internalize all the experiences of daily life. Mind you, wild Witches feel that dreams can be far more than just an elaborate subconscious filing system. Rather, we see them as a way for spirit guides and even the gods themselves to speak to us.

Here's a list of animal values (and a few insects) to consider when Nature's citizens appear in your night visions:

Aggressive animals:
           A perceived threat; unexpressed frustration or anger.

Animal carcass: Exposure; sense of being at the whims of fate; something "eating" at you.

Animals (variety): The wild within; our animal nature.

Ant: Fortitude; organization; community spirit; a new teacher or lesson.

Antelope: Not seeing the proverbial forest for the trees; try a new perspective.

Bat: Luck; joy; a message from the spirit world; guidance during "dark" times.

Bear: Grumpiness (acting bearish); forbearance; protection; fearlessness.

Bee: Medicine of the All; community; social interaction; teamwork; messages from spirits or the gods; creativity.

Bee (buzzing): Potential trouble on the horizon, or gossip.

Bluebird: Unequal joy and beauty.

Bird (caged): Loss of freedom or the illusion of freedom.

Bird (singing): A positive omen of victory or success.

Buffalo: Whatever you're working toward, stick to it. Don't give up now.

Bull: Obstinance; creativity or fertility; leadership qualities; ego.

Bull (taming): Keeping a powerful force under control.

Butterfly: Spiritual growth; esoteric awareness; new sense of self; happy relationships; rejuvenation.

Cat: Recuperative force; new beginnings; mystical energies; an alternative lunar emblem.

Chameleon: Blending into a situation; the ability to transform or recreate yourself; adaptability.

Chicken: Shyness or fear; the need for direction; matters of health (in the roost: the health of one's home and family).

Cow: Positive omen often portending nourishment (literal or figurative), also a symbol of the Great Mother.

Coyote: Some type of trickery or falsehood, so be wary.

Crab: Potentially the need for protection. If the crab is snapping its claws, consider your mood lately (have you been "crabby"?).

Crane: Vigilance; intellect; longevity.

Crocodile: Harsh words; deception; potential changes on the horizon (not always positive).

Crow: Don't stray from the course that you've set.

Deer: Surety; gentle naturedness. If a stag: the male aspect of the Universe.

Dog: Trustworthy friends and associates (if the dog is being gentle); having good instincts; devotion; honesty and trustworthiness.

Dolphin: The need for a quick decision or move; if leaping the need to catch your breath in a situation; joyfulness.

Dove: Peace; love; romance.

Dragonfly: Balance between thought and feeling; potential restlessness; good luck.

Duck: Marital happiness; cycles; instincts.

Eagle: Freedom; personal goals; strength of leadership qualities (note how high the eagle flies); pride.

Elephant: Devotion; gentle attention; awareness; kindness; wisdom; compassion; endurance; prudence.

Fish: Profuseness in an area of your life; fertility (usually physical); rejuvenation.

Fox: Craftiness; adaptability; the ability to blend in; potential hoax or fabrication.

Frog: Physical fertility; renewal (often of health); business improvements.

Goose: Creativity; good news enroute; potential goddess emblem; communication skills.

Hawk: Good perspectives: mental keenness; overcoming adversity (often physical).

Horse: Transitions; travel and movement; ambition.

Hummingbird: Happiness (often in love); truthfulness; live in balance.

Killing an animal: Purposeful banishing of something specific in your life. Consider what that animal represents.

Lion: Aggressiveness; bold communications; courage (especially in matters dealing with "demons" from the past); legal matters.

Lizard: A dream guide; good fortune; adaptability; psychic awareness; freeing yourself from an unhealthy or uncomfortable situation.

Lynx: A mystery solved or secret unveiled.

Monkey: Backsliding in your personal or spiritual development; unwise action; too much clowning around or flattery.

Mouse: Prudence; ingenuity; turning weaknesses into strengths; potential difficulties in communication.

Octopus: Potentially the wheel of time (especially with outstretched arms); misplaced or misapplied inventiveness.

Otter: Playfulness to the point of distraction; feminine energies entering your life.

Owl: Being true to self; sagacity in dark times; being watched by someone who does not have your best interests at heart; instinct (especially with matters affecting providence).

Parrot: Disparagement; a sham.

Peacock: False pride; a braggart (and a powerful one!).

Pelican: Giving all for love.

Pig: New beginnings; a treasure hidden in something distasteful.

Porcupine: A bristling personality; being overly defensive.

Rabbit: Fertility (usually physical); abundant energy; lunar influences.

Raccoon: Thievery; investigation.

Rat: The need to get your life in order (or a specific situation).

Robin: A new beginning filled with hope.

Sheep: Lacking self-confidence; being guided (possibly in the wrong direction).

Skunk: Making one's mark (often in a threatening situation); honor or recognition; irritation.

Snake: Transformation and growth; health.

Spider: Life's network; communication skills; tribe and family ties.

Swan:	Positively adapting to a new situation (and closing the old one).
Tiger:	Being a strong leader, dauntless, and intensely dedicated sometimes to the point of putting yourself in danger.
Turtle:	The need to withdraw to safety (often after taking on too much responsibility).
Venomous creatures:	
	What is trying to "poison" your outlooks?
Whale:	The beginning of a new, but difficult, course of action that will come out positively; renewal.
Wolf:	Feeling threatened by a person or situation; someone being untruthful; personal fears; cleverness.
Woodpecker:	The rhythm and cycle of life.

Putting all of this information together, say you dream of a lion eating an elephant. The lion is certainly the aggressor. Because the lion is devouring a symbol of kindness, that situation's or person's communications or approach toward you is completely overlooking your devotion and ongoing efforts. Alternatively, if YOU are the lion, consider where you might be overpowering someone in your life.

In another example, let's say you see yourself behind a wall with a bull waiting on the outside. This dream speaks of barriers. In this case it's between you and your stubborn nature. What are you being obstinate about to the point where it's actually impeding your progress?

Remember that dream interpretation is highly subjective. The meanings we've provided here are those found regularly in global dream keys, or those that come out of modern language usage (clever as a wolf, acting bearish, etc.). These are by no means all the interpretive values, so whenever possible we'd recommend comparing and contrasting this list to dream keys that you prefer and trust.

Modern Adaptation

Keeping in mind that many people live in urban environments where chance meetings and animal observations might prove very difficult, we'd like to offer some alternatives. There are other ways animal spirits, guides, and symbols can speak to your heart. They include repeated sightings of a creature (or its name) on or in:

- The media: TV, radio, Internet.
- Billboards.
- Advertising fliers.
- Business cards.
- Consumer products.
- Passing conversation.
- Gifts received.
- Patterns created by coffee grounds, rice, and so on.
- Food items brought home unexpectedly by housemates.

To provide an example: Perhaps during a week's time you see ads about a nature show on lions, notice a lion on a billboard, then hear someone talking about lions. As the saying goes, three's a charm. You might want to stop to consider what lion spirit is trying to tell you! Likewise, if your husband comes home with a surprise duck to cook for dinner, you notice a duck on a can of soup stock in your cupboard as you go to prepare the dish, and your dog shows up with his or her duck toy, I'd say Duck spirit is quacking for attention. And since you're already cooking, look to that "ritual" for aid. Traditionally ducks pertain to marital happiness, so why not consider preparing the duck with herbs that accent love, peace, joy, and devotion (a hint of basil, lemon, and honey on top with apple stuffing should do the trick!).

Beyond this approach you can certainly go to game farms, zoos, and even pet stores to observe animal behaviors. My only concern with this is that the creatures may or may not act "naturally" due to captivity. Consequently, the traditional interpretive values may be skewed. In this case I'd suggest going back to making an animal observation diary and using that to create interpretive values once you have enough data.

Chapter 4

Fur, Feather, and Fin: Spells and Charms

You never see animals going through the absurd and often horrible fooleries of magic and religion.... Dogs do not ritually urinate in the hope of persuading heaven to do the same and send down rain. Asses do not bray a liturgy to cloudless skies. Nor do cats attempt, by abstinence from cat's meat, to wheedle the feline spirits into benevolence. Only man behaves with such gratuitous folly.

—Aldous Huxley

Mr. Huxley's sentiments certainly weren't shared by the ancients. There was no sense of folly in their animal magick, nor in their reverence toward the powers of animal spirits. In fact, it is nearly impossible to read old collections of magick without seeing something contrived for animals (especially important farm animals). There are also thousands of spells that mention animal parts among the key constituents.

Historical Spells Utilizing Animal Parts or Symbols

Great writers and thinkers such as Pythagorus and Plotinus ruminated about animals having some type of spiritual essence. Meanwhile, for eons, common people and kings alike felt that the raw, wild power of a creature could be distilled somehow. Combining these two sentiments, it's easy to see why animal parts were utilized in ancient spellcraft.

With this in mind, we'd like to present a glimpse of some animals and how their images or parts were used in ancient magick around the world. The list that follows provides a broad-based overview of the potency that our ancestors trusted animal spirits to bear. Additionally, this list provides us with a starting place in considering how to use animal symbolism effectively in modern spells.

Adder: Hang the skin by the chimney to bring good luck; place skin in the rafters or the hearth to ensure protection against house fire.

Albatross:
In seafaring communities the found beak and skull of this bird was powdered and taken to cure disease. One could not simply kill the albatross to get its parts as that would bring a curse.

Alligator:
In South America an alligator tooth mounted in silver and gold and worn brings luck and safety.

Anaconda:
In South Africa images of the anaconda are used as apotropaic (intended to ward off evil) amulets.

Ants: Their eggs, eaten with honey, are believed to be an effective antidote to love.

Ass: The milk of a white ass was used in the Old Testament to designate and support nobility. Persian writings tell us that sleeping on this creature's skin keeps away nightmares and witchery, while wearing the right testicle on one's wrist brings love.

Badger: In the Far East people tattooed the image of a badger on their bodies in order to capture this creature's shapeshifting powers and to appease the rice spirit. The possession of a badger tooth is supposed to make a gambler unbeatable at any wager.

Bat: In Egypt, this was hung near pigeon houses to keep the birds from flying away. Europeans buried bats at crossroads with incense as part of love spells. The right eye of the bat kept in the waistcoat pocket is believed to make a person invisible. To kill a bat is to shorten one's own life span.

Bear: Various tribes buried a bear head with a deceased family member's body to keep them safe in the afterlife. Bears were sometimes killed as part of spells to appease vegetation spirits. In Syriac tradition placing the eye of a bear in a beehive brought prosperity. Finally, Romans wore bear images or claws to help with childbirth.

Beaver: In Europe, the testicles of this creature were thought to cure "diverse ills." Meanwhile, Zoroastrian priests might feed a beaver as part of a spell to bring rain or improve river food production.

Bee: The images of bees are found carved on tombs throughout the ancient world to protect the dead. They apparently convey the soul to the next world.

Blue jay: Feathers from these birds were a highly prized item for fetishes among the Ainu of Japan.

Boar: Among the Greeks boar teeth were worn on helmets for honor in battle, and boar meat was eaten at Olympic games to make sure no foul play occurred. The Celts put boar heads at graves to preserve the body from dangers and at the flesh to restore health and joy. Teutonic warriors wore boar-skin masks to help them uncover secrets or invoke Freyja's favor.

Bull: Alexandrians used bull testicles as fetishes, while the Sumerians employed them in weather magick. In Semitic tradition bull images were left at sacred sites to protect them.

Buzzard: In the Native American traditions of the Arizona and Mexican regions, buzzard feathers are often used to make the medicine man's garment to empower him.

Camel: In the Middle East, camel parts are used to cure rheumatism. The milk of a camel mixed with honey is an ancient love potion in Arabia. Additionally, its dung was used to combat hair loss, and the brain mixed with roses and applied was used to cure falling sicknesses.

Cat: In wish magick a stray whisker from a cat is very handy (note it has to be found, not taken). When you need your wish to manifest quickly, burn the whisker saying, "By my cat's whisker manifest my wish quicker."

Centipede:
             A traditional part of amulets to avert evil in China.

Chameleon:
             In a book of magick published in London in the 1800s, a fresh chameleon tongue insures legal success, the liver is eaten to hinder love charms, and powdered liver acts as an aphrodisiac.

Cicada: People in China sometimes keep these as pets for luck and longevity. Jade figurines are also placed in the mouth of a corpse to insure immortality.

Cock: Africans wore the claws of this creature as a protective amulet against fantastic animals such as the cockatrice. In both Greece and Scandinavia cocks were buried under the foundation of a building to protect it (specifically to keep away the spirit of death). White cocks were buried to turn away bad winds. At Hebrew weddings a cock and hen preceded the bride and groom to endow them with fertility. Cock blood feeds various spells and charms in both Santeria and Voodoo.

Cow: In Hindu tradition driving a cow across the threshold of a home brings plenty and fertility, and the urine may be used to cleanse a house after deaths or births.

Crane: In the Far East, carrying a white crane feather improves communication with the gods (it must be found, not taken).

Crocodile:
African Shamans use the liver in curses. Egyptians applied the dung to remove wrinkles (interestingly enough, in Egypt one of the crocodile's symbolic values is vanity and pride).

Crow: Aryans use the dung and urine in fertility spells, especially for new couples. In certain Native American customs giving a black feather of a crow was meant as a death curse.

Cuckoo: Pliny the Elder, a Roman scholar, encyclopedist, and author of *Historia Naturalis* (*Natural History*), states that these were used for ridding areas of fleas, and if the cuckoo was wrapped in hare hide, it would cure insomnia. In Europe, the egg of a cuckoo was part of fertility charms.

Deer: Powdered deer horn was used in medieval love spells and charms.

Dog: Hittites kept a dog figurine at important functions to banish evil. Peruvians did similarly, but buried the dogs near the threshold of homes or in tombs to act as guardians and guides. Greeks made offerings of a dog at crossroads to appease Hecate and avert hostile forces.

Eagle: The Toltec peoples carry the feather of an eagle to encourage a prayerful, contemplative attitude.

Egg: Rural tradition recommends breaking eggs into the land for a plentiful harvest.

Elk: Siberians use the hoof of an elk (the left hind foot) to cure vertigo, epilepsy, and other falling sickness.

Falcon: The Celts wore falcon talons to encourage a victory of spiritual energy over the carnal nature.

Fawn: In Greek Orphic tradition devotees wore fawn skin for protection and to honor Bacchus.

Fish: Among the followers of Ishtar, Isis, and Venus, fish was eaten regularly as part of spells for love and fecundity. Teutons likewise ate fish, but in this case it was to absorb their divine quality.

Frog: Egyptians carried frog-shaped amulets for health and placed them with mummies to represent new birth. Juvenal, a celebrated Latin poet and satirist, claims frog entrails were used as charms (they certainly appear in medieval medicaments). Whipping a frog was a medieval rain charm, and in Native American tradition this creature was part of many cleansing rituals. One example is that of placing a frog in a sick person's mouth, then sending the frog away so it would carry the sickness with it (thus the phrase "a frog in your throat"). Finally, in Europe a frog hung in white cloth was a love charm, and ashes of a frog mixed with tar cured baldness.

Goat: During the Roman Lupercalia Feast it was customary to wear a goat skin thong for fertility.

Goose: In England it was customary to eat goose on Michaelmas for luck.

Hare: In Greek tradition, carrying the rabbit's foot brings luck and fertility. In Japan if you wish to avert the evil eye you must find, scoop up, and turn over the tracks of a hare to turn the energy likewise away.

Hawk: In Borneo the feathers of this bird are used in healing spells.

Hen: The blood of a black hen was used in New England for a variety of external cures.

Hippo: Egyptians used the thigh of a hippo for virility magick.

Horse: Muslim tradition dictates that wearing horse hair shields the bearer from the evil eye, as do horseshoes.

Hyena: In Europe it was said that the skin of a male hyena, when inscribed with proper words and bound to the body, would protect against rabies.

Jaguar: In Central America images of jaguars were left at sacred sites for protection.

Kite: Greeks used a stick from this bird's nest as a cure for headaches.

Lion: Egyptians placed lion images at the gate of the temples for watchful protection and the land's continued fertility.

One-horned creatures (any):
Babylonians felt that making a cup from such a horn would neutralize all poisons (and thus protect the bearer from evil misdeeds).

Ostrich (feather and eggs):
African Bushmen carry eggs for their supernatural powers (specifically to find water) and the skin was quite valuable among Arabic people for spellcraft.

Otter: Wearing an otter's head in some Native American traditions invokes wisdom (more than likely due to the fact that the otter is among the trickster figures, and one must be wise to overcome him).

Owl: Among the Cherokee carrying an owl feather is said to improve night vision, and among the Pawnee it's protective especially in darkness. In West Africa the head of an owl was used for malevolent magicks.

Ox: Africans used the blood and gall from a black ox in rain-making spells.

Oyster: In some oceanic regions these are carried to help the bearer keep a secret.

Peacock: In China and Japan conferring a peacock feather on an individual gave him imperial favor.

Quail: In Greek tradition, the brain of this bird was sometimes used in an effort to cure epilepsy.

Raven: The head of a raven was used in Eskimo hunting magick to insure success.

Reindeer:
In Lapish tradition, spilling the blood of this creature insures good fortune for one's herds.

Red feather (any bird):
Among Polynesians, carrying one of these brings good luck (the feather has a talismanic quality).

Rhinoceros:
The horn of this creature (as well as other one-horned animals) will detect poison if used for beverages. In powdered form it was considered nearly a panacea for

everything from smallpox to stomachache in Greece and Arabia, while in the Far East it was a respected aphrodisiac.

Salmon: In Celtic superstitions, eating this fish confers wisdom and knowledge, and improves one's senses.

Scarab: These were buried in Egypt with bodies as amulets to restore the heart in the next world.

Seal: Romans believed donning sealskins would protect the wearer from thunderstorms.

Shark: People in Ceylon wore shark vertebrae on any part of their bodies to prevent cramps and disease.

Snake: Keeping pet snakes was common in Greece, Crete, and Rome in the belief that doing so brought health and fertility to all therein. Pliny mentions a belief that eating snake brings rejuvenation (but a cultural reference could not be found).

Sheep: West African medicine men sometimes use the eyelash of a sheep in malevolent magick.

Spider: Pliny tells us that swallowing a spider was a cure for jaundice, while putting one in a nutshell and carrying it was thought to overcome fever.

Stag: The Celts used various parts of the stag for therapeutic effects, probably due to this animal's symbolic value of overcoming evil.

Swallow: Swedes say this bird has two stones within it. If acquired the red one provides an instant cure, while the black one brings luck.

Swan: In Celtic tradition swan parts were used for therapies that were considered affected by the sun and water, often as a purifying energy. In sea-faring cultures a swan figurine carved into a masthead brings fair winds and protection at sea.

Swine: In Roman custom, a pig placed on an altar then ground into soil insured a rich harvest.

Tiger: The people of Ceylon used tiger whiskers for love potions and wealth amulets. Wearing the image of a tiger was a guard against disease, while drinking its pulverized bones cured nightmares in China.

Toad: Several ancient writers speak of a stone inside a toad's head, which once obtained, becomes a proof against poison. The skin of a toad was a recommended ingredient in heart elixirs, and as we now know, this skin contains a substance similar to digitalis.

Tortoise: In Japan if you whisper your wish to this creature, he will convey it to the sea god who (in turn) spreads the wish around the world through the waters.

Weasel: Salted flesh of weasel dipped in wine is an old folk remedy for a snakebite.

This list represents only a very small fraction of the suggested uses for animal images and parts that exist in folk medicine and magick (which often blend together, as shown here).

Everything Old Is New Again (Adapting Ancient Animal Spells)

We realize that there were a few entries in the previous section that probably made you a bit queasy. We live in very different times, with very different outlooks on our spirituality. So the question becomes, *How do we honor tradition without stepping over any boundaries (be those boundaries legal or personal)?* The legal portion of the question we answered in the last chapter. The personal one is something on which to meditate.

It's our considered opinion that with the exception of illegality, if someone finds a bone, feather, or other animal part he or she can consider it a gift from Nature or that specific animal spirit.

After all, the item wasn't purposefully hunted or harvested—it simply appeared. Our ancestors regarded such an occurrence as a blessing and usually put that gift to work somehow. Exactly how you choose to utilize that item is wholly a personal decision, but we don't see any reason NOT to use it in a spell or charm so long as proper health precautions are maintained.

> **WARNING: The material that follows regarding the proper cleaning of found animal parts is highly graphic in nature and may prove disturbing to some readers. However, we feel that this information is scientifically and sanitarily necessary. The intent is to make this process as safe as possible because decaying animal parts can (and often do) carry diseases harmful to humans. Please read and apply these materials with all due caution.**

Proper Preparation and Cleaning for Found Animal Parts

Feathers. In good condition, feathers should be placed in a freezer bag and put in the freezer for two to four weeks to kill any parasites. Feathers in poor (dirty) condition can be gently washed in a basin of soapy water, patted with a towel, and allowed to finish air drying before freezing.

Untanned furs. The endodermis should be scraped to remove all meat, fat, etc., then the hide can be washed in hot, soapy water, thoroughly rinsed, dried with a towel, and then stretched on a frame to complete drying. After fur is dried, it can be brushed. At this point, what a person has is a "raw-hided" piece of animal skin. The easiest way to tan the hide is to either have it tanned by a taxidermist, or buy a commercial tanning kit (it is possible to brain-tan, tannin-tan, alum-tan, urea-tan hides, but it requires more work and knowledge of animal skin preparation and care than the average person has, or wants to have!).

Tanned furs. Tanned furs can be sprinkled with cornmeal and brushed or vacuumed clean, or they can be taken to a drycleaners that specializes in leathers and furs. **Do not** wash tanned furs! The leather will become stiff and the fur may be damaged!

Bones. Bones without meat attached can be scrubbed well with soapy water and soak in a 10-percent Clorox solution (no more than 24 hours!) to whiten. Be certain to rinse the bones after the chlorox solution with fresh water and dry in a warm, sunny location (the windowsill is fine).

Bones. Bones with meat attached (including skulls) can be boiled in a pot of water until the meat starts loosening from the bones. Remove bones from boiling water and pick or scrub all meat from the bones. Continue as above.

Note: Skulls have a lot of cartilage (nasal area, skull plates) that helps to hold the skull together. Over-boiling will dissolve this cartilage, causing the skull to fall apart. Care should also be taken with the teeth, which will be loosened during the cleaning. Any loose areas on the skull can be glued later, after the skull has been bleached and thoroughly dried.

Legs, Wings, and Ears. Areas with little meat can be dried whole using silicon dioxide (most craft stores carry this chemical for drying flowers).

Nails and Claws. These are best removed from the animal and just washed in soapy water, rinsed, and allowed to air dry. It's important to remember that the nail-bone is sheathed in the removable claw covering: if you want to save the whole thing, you will have to cut the "finger" off (if you want to save some of the hide/hair around the nail, then use silicon dioxide to preserve it whole). Otherwise, after about a week of decay, the claw sheath will usually just slip off the nail-bone on its own. DO NOT put claws in chlorox: it will dissolve them!

Teeth. Teeth are very durable! They can be carefully removed from a fresh jawbone with a pair of pliers (just don't crush the tooth!). They can easily be removed from a boiled jawbone, and they normally can be pulled out of a decayed jawbone (a pocketknife is helpful to cut away the dried gums). As for cleaning, use soap, water, and chlorox (if desired). Normally, teeth are pretty clean; however, in cud-chewing animals (such as deer), plant material can be impacted in the molars, so remove this decaying material with a toothbrush, tweezers, toothpick, etc.

Eggs. The easiest way to clean fresh eggs is to make two small holes in the egg (one on either end) and blow the yolk out. This method does not work if there is a developing fetus inside the egg (in which case, blow out what you can and pour silicon dioxide into the egg to desiccate the fetal remains). Egg fragments (found in the woods after the chick has hatched) must be handled gently. I don't know of any way to harden the fragments, but you can certainly rinse these in soap and water.

Word of caution! Rabies is carried in the saliva of an animal. Domestic animals GET rabies. Wild animals CARRY rabies. Rabies can be contracted via contact with fur that has been licked by an animal with rabies. Rabies can also be transmitted via contact with the infected brain material. Animals also carry a wide variety of internal and external parasites. Animals found dead in the woods should be treated with extreme caution because they may be victims of rabies or distemper. Some animals, such as deer, can carry anthrax, which is transmittable to humans via contact with the infected liver (and by the time you've noticed that the internal organs look a little "odd," it's too late—you've already been exposed!). Things that can be transmitted (to humans and to domestic pets via human clothing) include, but are not limited to: mites, ticks, fleas, hookworm, tapeworm, roundworm, whipworm, rabies, anthrax, distemper (pets/animals only). **With this in mind, we strongly suggest you wear rubber gloves and avoid as much contact with your skin, hair, and clothing as possible during the collection and cleaning process. Afterward, thoroughly wash yourself and all clothing.**

Once you've followed these precautions, you may also wish to add a spiritual dimension and cleanse and purify the item for use in your magick. To this end, you can move it through purgative incense such as cedar or sage, sprinkle it with a bit of lemon-scented water (if that won't damage the piece), or perhaps say a prayer over it and thank the animal spirit for such a great treasure.

After you've completed the cleaning and cleansing process, there are several relatively easy ways to start using the animal parts for magick:

1. Carry the item as an amulet, talisman, fetish, or charm.

2. Make them into bracelets, earrings, and other wearable items that also double as portable power sources.

3. Wrap the item and place it where its energies are most needed (your altar).

4. Toss the item into a live water source (flowing) to carry the energy away or toward you.

5. Bury the item (for banishing) or with a live plant or seedling so energy "grows."

6. Dry and powder the item and use it in incense or other blends (make sure if you're going to burn it that it doesn't produce noxious fumes).

Putting this all together, let's look at several examples.

Black Feather: One day you find a simple black feather that catches your attention. You take it home and freeze it, not being wholly sure for what you'll eventually use it. A couple of weeks later you notice yourself feeling rather gloomy and forlorn. We suggest taking the feather to a moving water source (even a hose will do), focusing all your sadness into that feather, then letting the "blackness" float away from you. In this case, you've depended on the feather's color for symbolic value rather than the exact bird from which it came, which is perfectly acceptable!

Snakeskin: Over a week's time you notice a great deal of snake images as you travel around town and in the media. At the end of that week, you find a bit of snakeskin. It's definitely time to seriously consider what the snake spirit is telling you (you may have a totem here—see Chapter 8). But what about that bit of skin? Clean it up, following the guideline, then look up some of the metaphysical values for snakes in Appendix B and balance that information against your intuitive insights.

Cat's Claw: Trish periodically finds the sheath from one of her cat's claws caught in the carpeting. If it's from the cat that's her familiar, she blesses and charges it, and carries it as part of her power pouch. Otherwise, she stores it with other magickal goodies (this looks kind of nifty—having a storeroom that bears a resemblance to an old alchemist's lab!). In the future, when there's a situation where she needs to get back on her feet or recoup somehow, it is an ideal time to utilize the claw in a spell. In this case, she grinds it fine and adds it to powder for her shoes so she can literally land on her feet!

Deer Bone: If you happen to have a deer totem, this is a great item to simply keep on your altar to honor the creature. Otherwise, a found piece of antler makes for a wonderful set of runes when sliced and etched. Better still, because the deer has associations with gentleness, your rune readings will be communicated with a "gentle" voice. Alternatively, carry the bone with you as a charm on those days when you need a calmer demeanor!

Bird's Egg: You find a good-sized portion of a bird's egg and are in the midst of starting a new project. Bury that egg remnant with something that represents your project nestled neatly inside. Over that spot, put something that blossoms so your energy in this new endeavor is likewise protected and flourishing.

In these five examples you can see that the way you apply the symbolic value of a found item needs to match the goal of the magick. If your symbolism and purpose are antithetical, the spell is likely to go awry, if it works at all. Additionally, the symbolism MUST make sense to you personally. You need to trust in your magickal processes and the animal spirit, as faith and willpower drive the energy toward manifestation.

What happens to those wild Witches who decide they do not wish to use actual animal parts (either in one particular situation or all the time)? In this case, it's important to remember that within the construct of a sacred space, an object is every bit as powerful as what it represents. This means we can look to symbolic representations to take the creature's place.

Historical writings from around the world provide illustrations of animal imagery being used rather than a live creature. In particular, we see it in crystal and stone amulet and charm creation (the idea being that stone is very durable, so the magick would last longer). For example, Egyptians carried cat carvings to protect themselves from spells; Malaysian Witches used cat claws for strength talismans; and in Japan, the image of a cat with its paw raised is a common charm for luck and prosperity. A 13th century Hebrew text suggests carving a falcon on topaz to insure the goodwill of leaders and judges, a lion on garnet for honor and protection, a ram on sapphire to cure disease, and a bat on bloodstone to increase the power of magickal incantations! Finally, some anonymous 14th century writings go on to recommend carving a jasper with the image of a dog or stag and carrying it to heal insanity.

Other than stones, here are some other media in which you can find animal images:

- Small figurines.

- Metal charms.

- Pictures from magazines or old encyclopedias (check secondhand bookstores).

- Paintings.

- Product labels.

- Buttons, pins, and beads.

- Children's toys and game parts.

- Playing cards (with wildlife images on the back).

- Clay, wood, paper (on which you write or carve the creature's name).

Most folks will be looking for a specific animal image for a similarly specific magickal goal. Try to choose your media and an image so that both supports that goal. For example, if you want the image of a bear so you can banish your "bearish" attitude, I wouldn't spend a fortune on a metal charm or stone carving of a bear. Instead, look to paper, which is easily disposable and ecologically friendly!

Spells for Animal Companions

The concept of protecting the important creatures in our lives is nothing new. If we look to the Celts as one example, farmers would drive their cattle through the smoke of a bale fire annually to keep them safe from disease. Other examples include:

- ✱ Planting elder around one's home was common to keep the animals safe within. Note that the tree needs to remain undisturbed by animals or humans to provide this power (European/American).

- ✱ Dabbing a white substance between the animal's eyes to ward off the effects of the evil eye upon them (Hebrew).

- ✱ Putting bells on the creature's collar. The bells we still see on many pet collars date back to the time when bells were trusted to keep away malevolent spirits.

- ✱ Placing elderflowers near where the creature spends most of its time to prevent illness (European/American).

- ✱ Placing the image of an inverted crescent moon on the animal's collar for protection (Greeks did this for cats, specifically).

- ✱ Buttering an animal's paws is an old Scottish custom to keep a pet from wandering.

With this in mind, let's put together a few spells for beloved animal companions.

Health

Perhaps the best way to encourage the health of a creature is by allowing them to internalize positive magick through blessed food or water (the food, however, has to be something that's actually good for the animal in question). Take whatever you've chosen and add some veterinarian recommended powdered vitamins to it. Stir three times clockwise to generate beneficial, healthful energies while repeating each time:

> *Thrice round and round the sacred wheel, bless*
> *with energies that protect and heal.*

Protection

Find a small bell that you can hang from the animal's cage, tank, or collar. Try to find one that has a gold-tone to it. Gold is the sun's color, which confers protective energy and blessings. Dab a bit of fennel water on this (the scent that also deters fleas). Focus on the type of protection you wish to give this animal, saying:

> *Ring loud and true, this golden bell; with a*
> *warning ring and tell; ever keep* _____
>   *(the creature's name)*   *safe and well.*

Put it in the intended location. By the way, if the creature has a very "close call" with illness, accident, or death, it's a good idea to recharge the bell or get a new one to revitalize the energy.

Rapport and Love

To encourage growing rapport and love between you and your animal companions, we suggest making something for the animals with your own hands. For example, Trish embroidered a little pink heart on her cat's collar. Whatever you make, it should be something the animal can use or wear regularly. While you work, visualize your love for that animal as a pink-white light pouring into the token. When you're done, bless the item before giving it to your companion by saying:

> *As within so without, as below so above,*
> *into this token I place my respect and my love.*

Wanderlust

To follow the Scottish custom to keep your cat or dog from wandering away, put a little oleo on its paws (which neatly also combats furballs). As you dab each paw, recite an incantation such as,

No matter where you roam,
always safely return home!

Now that you have a better feel for how the wild Witch integrates animal parts and symbols into his or her spell craft, we can take the next step and consider other magickal processes. See, the animal spirit is not limited to any one part of our magickal or mundane lives. If we allow it, we can let those energies touch, bless, and inspire us every day, everywhere we go.

Chapter 5

The Circle of Life: Animals in Ritual

*In the Native American tradition...a man,
if he's a mature adult, nurtures life. He does
rituals that will help things grow, he helps raise
the kids, and he protects the people. His entire
life is toward balance and cooperativeness. The
ideal of manhood is the same as the ideal of
womanhood. You are autonomous, self-
directing, and responsible for the spiritual,
social and material life of all those with whom
you live.*

—Paula Gunn Allen

Throughout the world people use ritual and ceremonies
to mark important moments in life. The birth of a child, the
death of an elder, a marriage, coming of age for a youth—each
of these occasions and many more have become the focus of
personal and communal rituals, in part to commemorate all the
occasions and feelings that make us human. Each reenactment
of ritual gives it greater familiarity to the people gathered,
and celebrates their unity as a "tribe" (be it a tribe of culture

or choice). Ritual also honors that tribe's beliefs in a very potent way that touches the hearts of the whole, as well as the individual.

While it's true that rituals are dramatically different depending on the era and group represented, the core of ritual remains the same. Formal religious ritual is a way of fulfilling our connection to the world of Spirit. Here, in a sacred space devised by our own hands, we put aside the mundane world for a while and focus wholly on our role as wild Witches.

What is Ritual for Wild Witches?

By definition, *ritual* is:

1) The prescribed form or order of conducting a religious or solemn ceremony. 2) A series of such acts. 3) Any habitual detailed method of procedure. *(The Tormont Webster's Illustrated Encyclopedic Dictionary)*

Rituals for wild Witches are all about creating coherency and honoring the patterns of our life. The goal of a ritual is to create a cohesive outline into which we can pour our energy. From that point forward, the pattern grows outward or inward (or both) for manifestation. The main difference between rituals in this construct and those you walk through every day is the religious element involved.

Don't let the religious element deter you. The word ritual naturally makes people a little uneasy because humans as a whole are not accustomed to the idea of taking on the role of priest or priestess in their lives. Truthfully, however, we already do so each time we make an ethical choice. In the wild Witch's worldview, you have the right and responsibility to remain an active participant in your spiritual fulfillment. That means either working ritual on your own; creating them yourself; or enacting them with a group of like-minded people, remaining fully aware of that spark of the God and Goddess down deep in your soul.

Every ritual will be slightly different depending on the "whys" that a practitioner previously determined. This also means that the focus of the ritual, the individuals involved, and the tradition represented all play a part in the words, tools, symbols, timing, and overall environment of any ritual. Wild Witches strive for life-affirming, transformative rituals, and the ability to bring one's vision and tradition into the mix is nothing less than essential.

No matter the "whys" or "whens" (or even the "wheres") of ritual, the most important thing is that we *do* ritual...that we make that attempt to reconnect with one another and with the Divine. Wild Witchery recognizes the significance ritual plays in our own lives, and its impact on our social customs and cultures. Rituals help to define who we are, as individuals, as a people, and as a future.

But how does all this relate to animal magick, specifically? In the ritual circle animal carvings and paintings might symbolize the four elements: perhaps a fish for Water or a bird for Air. Animal spirits can be called upon to guard the sacred space as appropriate to each quarter, such as calling on a lizard for the South.

Living animals can come into the circle to keep us alert and aware of various energies, or to enjoy the magick. Some animals, such as dogs, can even learn to help create the sacred space by walking with their masters. Really, the options are as endless as your imagination.

Spirit Guardians and Watchtowers

Let's get more specific about how to blend the ideas and symbols from wild Witchery into a rite. One of the first ways in which you can bring animal spirits into the equation is by using specific creatures to represent the four quarters of the sacred space.

Animals did not escape the human tendency toward metaphysical classifications. Historically, each creature was aligned with a particular element and associated attributes. Most often the elemental category depended on habitat. This correspondence was important in folk healing when applying the law of similars (a water creature's parts might be used to cure a fever, for example).

Here are some examples of traditional correspondences for you to consider in setting up your sacred space, with Native American associations in parenthesis after the element's name:

- 🦋 Air (creatures that fly): Most birds, flying fish, butterfly, dragonfly, ladybug, bee, and many other winged creatures.

- 🐎 Fire (creatures that creep): Scorpion, lion, lizard, horse, desert creatures, electric eel, and many creatures with a fiery sting.

- 🐦 Water (creatures that swim): Fish, seahorse, dolphin (can also be Air), seal, walrus, crab, seagull, whale, duck, beaver.

- 🦌 Earth (creatures that walk): Snake, rabbit, cow, gopher, bear, deer, mole, ferret, mouse, and many forest dwelling creatures.

In putting this together for Circle, we suggest carefully choosing the animal spirits so that their energies work well together. Natural predators to one another may not "play nicely" with each other in the sacred space any more than gods or goddesses from different cultures might. For example, we're not sure how comfortable the Circle would be if Bear spirit held the North and Fish spirit held the West, because Bear might be hungry!

We point this out not to dissuade you from calling on animal spirits as guardians, but to remind you that animal spirits still bear all their natural tendencies and attributes. We cannot wholly predict the behavior of such beings any more so than we can devas. Both embody raw drives and motivations that are often foreign to humans.

With this in mind, it's best to develop relationships with specific animal spirits and guides before calling on them to guard the sacred space. This approach is also more respectful to these beings. Just as you would not ask favors from a god or goddess with whom you haven't developed a relationship, the same holds true here. A wild Witch honors Nature's powers and never assumes that animal spirits are ours to randomly command as if they were lesser beings, or children. Any Shaman will tell you that you're in for a rude awakening if you take that tact.

That caveat aside, once you have several animal spirits with whom you interact, they will likely enjoy joining you in the sacred space. Returning to our previous example of an invocation, in this instance, rather than calling on a nameless watch-tower and its Elemental energy, you'd be inviting a specific animal spirit. For example, if you've chosen Bee to guard the East you might say,

> *Hail Bee spirit, guardian of the East and Air.*
> *Come, join me/us in this sacred space, bringing*
> *with you the honey of creativity.*

The beauty of inviting your animal spirits and guides into the space is that it provides a valuable opportunity to work in partnership with these spirits. It also sets aside time wherein you become more intimately aware of their energy patterns. Feeling the way in which animal spirits hold their quarter, and listening to any messages they choose to impart, continues the process of relationship-building that's so important to successful animal magick.

Altar Animals

Another way to honor your animal spirits and guides is by including them on your altar in the sacred space. Here, small statues, paintings, images from magazines, or even origami can sit as a way of either showing appreciation for your totems, or as a way of showing respect toward a god or goddess who holds that creature as sacred.

Nearly every god or goddess is associated with a specific animal in their regional folktales or mythologies. Sometimes the animals are companions for the god or goddess, sometimes they are an important part of the deity's history, and periodically, the Divine Being shapeshifts himself or herself into an animal for a particular purpose.

For those of you who might like to include animal imagery to please a god or goddess, here's a brief list of some global deities and the animals they're thought to protect. This list is especially useful when working magick for your pets or other earthly creatures because you can call on a god or goddess who is appropriate to the task (such as calling on Bast to help a feline companion). It's also useful to know what gods and goddesses hold your totems and guides in high regard.

Akupera (Hindu):	Tortoise whose back supports the world.
Amaterasu (Japan):	Sun goddess to whom crows are sacred.
Amun (Egypt):	Sun god who favors any hatched creature; cows.
Anubis (Egypt):	Guide for souls to whom dolphins and jackals are sacred.
Aphrodite (Greek):	Goddess of love who protects dolphins, goats, and swans.
Apollo (Roman):	God of light and the arts, who oversees magpies, horses, and pure breeds.
Arachne (Greek):	Spider goddess, weaver of fate.
Arduinna (Gaulish):	Goddess of hunting whose sacred animal was a boar.
Aristaeus (Greek):	Protector of flocks and beekeeper.

Artemis (Greek): Moon goddess to whom bears, fowl, and all wild animals are sacred.

Artio (Gaulish): Goddess of forests and hunting whose attribute is a bear.

Athena (Greek): Goddess of art and war often depicted with a snow owl, peacock, or eagle.

Atergatis (Syrian): Fertility goddess and guardians of fish and snakes.

Avilayoq (Inuit): God who protects seals, whales, and all sea creatures.

Bast (Egypt): Cat-faced goddess of joy.

Benten (Japan): A love goddess with snake and dragon aspects.

Blodeuwedd (Welsh): Flower-faced goddess to whom owls are sacred.

Bullai-Bullia (Australian Aborigine):
Goddess who has the form of a parrot.

Candra (India): Moon god whose chariot is pulled by white horses or an antelope.

Chenti-irti (Egypt): Falcon god sometimes identified with Horus.

Chingchinich (Native American):
God who appears as a coyote.

Diana (Rome): Goddess of nature under whose dominion lies the dog and elephant.

Djata (Borneo): Water dwelling goddess who has crocodiles as servants.

Dyaus (India): Sky god sometimes depicted as a bull or cow.

Fatit (Albanian): Destiny Beings who appear as butterflies.

Finn (Ireland): Hero who often appears as a stag.

Ganymede (Greek): Cup bearer who oversees eagles and peacocks.

Garuda (Indian): Prince of birds and servant of Vishnu.

Hannahanna (Hittite): Goddess of childbirth who is served by bees.

Hunapu (Guatemalan):
Protector god to whom bats are sacred.

Isis (Egypt): Great goddess who is often depicted with an owl, lion, or snake.

Isara (Mesopotamian):
Queen of judgement and witness to oaths. Her emblems were the scorpion, snake, and lizard.

Legba (West African): Divinatory god who uses a dog as a messenger.

Loki (Scandinavian): Trickster god who protects similarly crafty animals such as the fox.

Lunonnatar (Finland):
Creation goddess who oversees egg-laying creatures.

Mari (Celtic): Poetic sea goddess to whom water animals, rams, and crows are sacred.

Mbotumbo (Ivory Coast):
Protective god with an ape head.

Odin (Scandinavian): God of wisdom and cleverness whose animals are raven and horse.

Para (Finland): Domestic spirits who can appear as snakes, frogs, or cats.

Preas Eyn (Khmer): God who corresponds to Indra who rides a three-headed elephant.

Ratnasambhava (China): A Dhyani-Buddha, his cart is drawn by a pair of lions and a horse.

Sadhbh (Irish): Goddess who protects deer and often appears as one.

Sequana (Gallic): Goddess of the River Seine to whom ducks are sacred.

Shou Lao (China): God of long life whose symbol is the white crane.

Tnong (Malacca Peninsula): A sun god who takes the shape of a dragonfly.

Toeris (Egypt): Protective goddess with the body of a hippopotamus.

Turan (Etruscan): Love goddess whose attributes include the dove and swan.

Usanas (India): Regent of the planet Venus sometimes portrayed sitting on a camel.

Veive (Etruscan): God who has a goat attribute.

WI (Sioux): Sun god to whom bison are sacred.

Yu-qiang (China): God of the sea who has a fish body and rides two dragons. When he's commanding ocean winds, he becomes a bird.

This list represents but a very small portion of the gods or goddesses with animal attributes. The fact that animals were so strongly connected with the Divine implies the reverence the ancients had toward them. It also speaks strongly of the connection that our ancestors saw between Nature and the gods.

Animal Ambiance

Now that your altar is suitably decorated, don't stop there! Look to the whole of the sacred space and consider what other touches you could add to make the whole experience multi-sensual. For example, if you're honoring animal spirits at the four Quarters, why not play a nature CD or tape as you get to those Quarters that reflect the animal's environment? Or you could have nature sounds playing throughout the ritual. Or if the animals with which you're working are all tropical, try hanging some jungle-styled curtains on the wall and setting up a humidifier to make the room moist and warm.

Here are some other ideas for helping to round out the ritual experience:

* Using natural-scented incense (such as pine for forest-dwelling animals).

* Enacting a mime of the various animal spirits on which you're calling to better connect with their energy.

* Putting images of the animals at eye level so you can easily visualize them throughout the rite.

* Having plants native to the creature on the altar or inside the sacred space at the appropriate Quarter.

* Wearing a fabric whose texture reminds you of the animal's fur.

⚼ Marking the edge of the sacred space with items that reflect the animal spirits on which you're calling. For example, if working with aviary creatures, use cornmeal or birdseed as the boundary (something that naturally attracts birds).

⚼ Utilizing enclosed flame or fake fire rather than candles (many animals fear fire).

⚼ Having an elemental medium that honors the creature. For example, if the animal is saltwater-dwelling, invoke it in the West and have salt water in that region as opposed to fresh.

None of these options makes for a ritual that's much more complicated, it's simply more thoughtful. By taking this extra step, every motion and medium in your sacred space uplifts the spirits on which you're calling for insights or aid.

Living Creatures in the Sacred Space

Many wild Witches enjoy having pets or familiars with them in the sacred space. Mind you, we'd be hard-pressed to keep them out! There's something about magickal energy that naturally attracts our animal companions to it. Whenever Trish is doing an auric balancing on someone, for example, the cats roll around on the floor nearby gleefully. They will rub all over, walk on top of, and generally make a nuisance of themselves around the person to whom the energy is directed. She takes this as a "sign" that the energy is flowing correctly; if it were not, the animals wouldn't respond so positively.

How do wild Witches create a sacred space that's acceptable for their animal companions, and what roles do the animals play, if any, during the ritual? Well, the primary concern is safety. Cats in particular seem to be fascinated by a dancing candle flame (which usually leads to seared whiskers). Long-haired dogs (or ones with long tails) can pose similar safety issues if you have a brazier or open flame near the floor. So, the first consideration here is safe placement of any candles or incense (safe, in this case, meaning well out of jumping range).

The next consideration is the use of herbs, beverages, and any other edible items during the ritual. Most pampered pets *love* human food. If they see *their* human consuming something, it stands to reason that they'll want a bite. Unfortunately, some of the things we consume are not healthy for our animals, and some herbs in particular are downright lethal if consumed in large enough quantity. Please do your research. For example, chocolate, lily, chrysanthemum, mistletoe, and onions are bad for cats. Aloe, holly, lily, chocolate, poinsettia, salt, and mushrooms cause problems with dogs. If you want your familiar or companion to stay healthy, it might be best to leave such items out of the ritual (or perhaps substitute something better for the creature). Mistletoe, for example, is sometimes used for protection. For both cats and dogs, however, garlic is a better choice because it also deters fleas.

A third safety issue is the use of athames or other sharp implements. While the symbolism of the sacred knife as being able to bless or curse is nice, it's not necessarily wise to have a sharp blade around unpredictable animals that may perceive the item as a threat. We'd suggest a wand or even your pointer finger to direct energy as options here.

Fourth, look at the entirety of your sacred space for issues from the pet's perspective. Is the region in which they'll be sitting, walking, or whatever, clean and free of debris and distraction even as you would want in your own sacred space? If you're blessing the participants with smudge when they enter the space, how will the animal receive the blessing so that it won't frighten them? If you're having a post ritual feast, do you have snacks for the animal, too? So long as you perceive the living creature in your space as a valuable spiritual partner and treat him or her with appropriate respect, you'll do just fine on these points.

The question still remains of what the pet will be doing in the sacred space. The answer depends much on the animal. Some will just wish to enjoy the ambiance and not get involved more than lying there and sharing energies. Other animals, however, want more active roles. Dogs in particular can be trained to walk the perimeter of the Circle with a master or mistress and help invoke the Watchtowers. They can also be taught to guard a particular Quarter of the space. As with any type of animal training, this takes some time, patience, and positive affirmation for the pet, but it's very feasible.

What's really neat about an animal that actively participates in ritual is the fact that it supports everything that wild Witchery represents in fundamental terms. Namely, it says we're honoring Nature and its energies; we're honoring the animals that share our lives as more than mere pets over which to rule, and we're expressing our love toward both the earth and our animal companions by trusting their instincts and wanting them with us in the working of magick.

Chapter 6

Zodiac and Beyond: Astrological and Celestial Animals

Astrology: do we make a hullabaloo among the stars, or do they make a hullabaloo down here?

Our zodiac here is the life of man in one round chapter.... To begin: there's Aries, or the Ram—lecherous dog, he begets us; then, Taurus, or the Bull—he bumps us the first thing; then Gemini, or the Twins—that is, Virtue and Vice; we try to reach Virtue, when lo! comes Cancer the Crab, and drags us back; and here, going from Virtue, Leo, a roaring Lion, lies in the path—he gives a few fierce bites and surly dabs with his paw; we escape, and hail Virgo, the virgin! that's our first love; we marry and think to be happy for aye, when pop comes Libra, or the Scales—happiness weighed and found wanting; and while we are very sad about that, Lord! how we suddenly jump, as Scorpio, or the Scorpion, stings us in rear; we are curing the wound, when whang come the arrows all

round; Sagittarius, or the Archer, is amusing
himself. As we pluck out the shafts, stand aside!
here's the battering-ram, Capricornus, or the
Goat; full tilt, he comes rushing, and headlong
we are tossed; when Aquarius, or the
Waterbearer, pours out his whole deluge and
drowns us; and, to wind up, with Pisces, or the
Fishes, we sleep.

—Herman Melville

Any book about animals would be remiss to overlook the bestiary that sparkles in the sky. Western astrology began some time around 2000 B.C.E. in the region of Babylon. By 1600 B.C.E. there were tables that chronicled more than 7,000 astrological omens, and by 410 B.C.E. the earliest horoscope appeared on the Cylinder of Gudea (now residing at Oxford).

While the earliest astrology acted as a visual map for travelers and an agricultural guide, natal astrology as a predictive method appeared by 5 B.C.E. Eudoxus, a Greek astronomer, reintroduced the idea in the 4th century A.D., but it never really caught on until later in history. No matter the purpose of the study, however, the early astrological correspondences were based on the five-planet system (Mercury, Venus, Mars, Jupiter, and Saturn), the sun and the moon.

No matter the era or setting, throughout both the social and metaphysical systems of astrology, the ancients told grand stories about natural and mythical animals, as patterned by the stars above. How do these images affect magickal practices? What do the Chinese and Western astrological calendars tell us about animal symbolism? This chapter shares ideas on how you can use celestial creatures to improve both everyday life and spiritual pursuits.

[The word horoscope comes from the Greek]
[*horuos skopos* meaning "time observer."]

Creature Features

Many constellations get their name from animals or myths about animals. In Western astrology, seven out of the 12 birth signs bear animal imagery. That equates to nearly 60 percent of the entire predictive system!

Wild Witches may or may not use astrology as a predictive personal system to guide daily actions. More commonly, they turn to moon signs for consideration in timing their spells and rituals. While timing isn't typically necessary to wild Witchcraft, it is a supportive system that has a long and respected history among Mages in many cultures.

What we're presenting here is a sampling of both the personal predictive system and the magickal applications for your consideration (bearing in mind that we are only covering the seven signs depicting animals, as applicable to this book):

Aries, March 21–Aril 19

A person born under this sign tends to have a very strong, pioneering spirit. The Ram spirit likes to lead, explore, and invent. In relationships, Aries are best mated with Leo or Sagittarius. Famous Rams include Bach and Descartes.

When a person has planets in the Ram's house, it dictates various aspect of his or her personality. For example, a person with Pluto in Aries reveals someone who is very independent and somewhat secretive with others, whereas someone with Mars in the same location will be a very competitive leader.

When the moon is in Aries it's the ideal time to perform magick for improved motivation, enthusiasm, breaking down barriers, and cleansing.

Taurus, April 20–May 20

A person born under this sign tends to be dedicated and faithful, sometimes to a fault. The bull-headed nature of this sign makes for a stick-to-it-to-the-bitter-end attitude. On a more positive note, those working with Bull energies are often very artistic. For a good relationship, Taurus should look to Virgo or Capricorn. Famous Bulls include Barbara Streisand and Dante Gabriel Rossetti.

When a person has planets in the Bull's house it dictates material possessions. For example, if you have Neptune here, it portends the desire to collect religious items, or the ability to make money from religious-oriented activities.

When the moon is in Taurus, consider working magick aimed toward abundance, productivity, and tenacity.

Cancer, June 22–July 21

A person born under the sign of the crab tends to be somewhat of a homebody, who is both cautious and creative. If you want someone to remember an important piece of information or protect some treasure, Cancers will tuck either neatly in a claw and hang on to it until you tell them otherwise (making them great economists). In relationships Cancer should seek out Pisceans or Scorpios. Famous Crabs include Ann Landers and Diana Rigg.

When a person has planets in Cancer, it rules matters of home and security. For example, a person with Saturn located in this house would likely value honesty with those he loves, and find security in his own sense of duty.

Magickally speaking, when the moon is in Cancer, consider enacting spells or rituals directed toward inventiveness and fruitfulness.

Leo, July 22–August 21

The Lion spirit roars loudly in this birth sign, creating people who are courageous and prideful. Leos tend to be financially fortunate, and they like it that way. They also prefer to work in very visible positions where the ego gets some needed stroking. Lions mingle well in relationships with Aries or Sagittarius. Famous Lions include Helena Blavatsky and Alexander Dumas.

When a person has planets in the Lion's house it rules children and hobbies (playtime). For example, if one has Mercury in this house the person is likely to enjoy logical games, such as chess.

When the moon is in Leo it's a good time to work spells and rituals focused on developing new personal abilities or strengths.

Scorpio, October 23–November 21

The typical person born under the sign of Scorpio will be ingenious, determined, introspective, changeable, prideful, and highly competitive. They tend to be people of extremes, being charming one moment and stinging like the Scorpion the next. Good mates for Scorpio are Pisceans and Cancers, and famous Scorpios include Martin Luther and Pablo Picasso.

When a person has planets in this house, it rules over matters of learning, science, and travel. For example, a person with Venus in this house might prefer personal pleasure to studies.

When the moon is in Scorpio it supports magick directed toward passion, expressing one's sexuality, learning, and uprooting negativity.

Capricorn, December 22–January 20

People born under the sign of the Goat are devoted, very practical, and disciplined. They tend to have tremendous patience, strong convictions, and display good negotiating skills thanks to a keen understanding of methodology. In other words, it's hard to get a Capricorn's proverbial "goat"! Capricorn's best mates are people born under Taurus or Virgo. Famous Goats include Alexander Hamilton and Isaac Asimov.

When a person has planets in this house, it rules over matters of honor, goals, and personal status. Consequently, someone with Uranus in this house might receive personal honors for some type of service they provide regularly.

Magikally, when the moon is in Capricorn, consider enacting spells and rituals aimed at harvesting the fruits of your labors and inner development.

Pisces, February 20–March 20

People born with the Fish spirit ruling their lives will typically be very flexible, generous, and caring (sometimes to a fault). These friendly dreamers are the "mommies" of the Zodiac, and will often swim upstream to fight for a cause or help a friend, even if they drown trying. They also find it difficult to balance their spiritual thirst with mundane life. Pisces should pair with Libra or Gemini in relationships. Famous Fish include Michelangelo and Einstein.

When a person has planets in this house, it rules over hidden matters, enemies, and retribution. For example, someone with Mars in this house will simply take up the sword and boldly fight for their rights, whereas someone with Pluto here would do their fighting from a well-hidden location.

When the moon is in Pisces, it supports magick for positive progress, movement, improved psychism, and even the occasional miracle.

Pet Personalities and Astrology

We've talked about how the creature features sparkling in night the sky affect human life, but what about animal life? What type of personality can you expect in your cat or dog if they're born under the influence of animal signs? First let's consider feline companions:

Aries: Ram-born cats demand the attention they feel they are most certainly due. For the budget-minded pet owner, however, these felines tend to be very healthy (we think they're just trying to avoid vet visits).

Taurus: Where the Aries cat wants attention, the bull-headed feline *gets* it, even if it means tripping their unaware human on the way to the bathroom. As a distraction, try giving him or her a colorful, shiny toy (Taurus is the "blond" sign of the cat world).

Cancer: If you're planning to have an outdoor cat, don't get one born under the sign of the Crab. This kitty wants to be indoors. Additionally, Crab-cats reach out with their claws to *one* human and will be fiercely devoted to that person throughout their lives.

Leo: Oh, my—a cat born under the Lion—talk about a proud and arrogant pussy! Do not expect this cat to be anywhere but the top of the pecking order. And forget even trying to feed Lion-kitty that generic dry food. Only gourmet will do.

Scorpio: This cat is happiest in a one-pet home (meaning her home, of course!). As a psychic partner, Scorpio cats can't be beat. Trust their instincts and you won't be disappointed.

Capricorn: The tidiest, most purr-snikety cat in the universe, don't disrupt the Goat-cat's sense of order and make sure her litter box is immaculate unless you want an unpleasant surprise.

Pisces: A cat born under the influence of a fish—how embarrassing! This kitty is moody and often lacks the typical cat confidence. Expect the items with which they're fascinated to change moment-to-moment. The best "toy" for this cat is a fish tank to gaze upon.

And here's the corresponding list for our Canine companions:

Aries: This puppy's mantra is "throw the ball, throw the ball!" She thrives on playful attention, and doesn't take well to being left alone for long periods of time.

Taurus: For a bulldog, you couldn't ask for a better sign. She will be filled with pride and unbridled joy. For other canines, Taurus seems to inspire a youthful demeanor and desire for *lots* of affection.

Cancer: If you're looking for a dog that embodies the phrase "man's best friend," find a pup born under this sign. However, be aware that she will want to be with you everywhere and anywhere.

Leo: A dog born under a cat's sign is the laughing stock of the canine world. To make up for this embarrassment, Lion dogs will ritualistically mark their territory and that of every other dog within a three-mile radius. The only region in which this isn't true is in Buddhist households where the image of a Lion dog is honored as symbolic of balance and sacred law.

Scorpio: Dogs born under the Scorpion have incredibly sharp instincts. They're good protectors, and also make excellent watchers and familiars for wild Witches.

Capricorn: A dog that loves having her own doghouse (with a soft mattress, please), and who will never wander far from that space. If you have to move any time during this canine's life, expect trauma.

Pisces: If you want an independent, aloof dog, this is the sign for which to watch. However, the Piscean dog is generally happier as part of a dog pack than associating with humans.

As with all divinatory arts, these are broad generalizations only and, in this case, presented solely for your amusement.

Chinese Animal Astrology

Chinese astrology, while based on similar concepts as Western forms, varies in its techniques and interpretive values, specifically the signs are all animal oriented. An ancient myth tells how Buddha designed the 12 signs in this system just prior to his ascension. Before leaving Earth, he wished to see all the animals, but only 12 answered his invitation.

First to arrive at Buddha's bash was the Rat, who loved social occasions. The Ox came next, being very timely. Tiger made an entrance after this, wishing to be the center of attention (never arrive too early to a party or there's no one to see you!). Cat followed, having been waylaid by a mouse. Dragon came fifth, bringing all types of energy with him. Snake was sixth, hoping to charm all the guests, while Horse quietly entered seventh, offering assistance to his host. The Goat was eighth, and fully planned to be a show-off all night, but Monkey stole the show, entering center stage ninth. Rooster reaches the celebration 10th, thinking to get great attention with his crowing. Dog, not wishing to rush, arrived 11th, and finally the Boar (who overslept from his last party) arrived last. Buddha promised to name successive years after each of these animals. He went on to say that people born during those years would bear the animals' traits.

To determine your animal signs refer to the following chart:

Birth Year	Animal
1960, 1972, 1984, 1996, 2008, 2020	Rat
1961, 1973, 1985, 1997, 2009, 2021	Ox (or Buffalo)
1962, 1974, 1986, 1998, 2010, 2022	Tiger
1963, 1975, 1987, 1999, 2011, 2023	Cat (or Rabbit)
1964, 1976, 1988, 2000, 2012, 2024	Dragon
1965, 1977, 1989, 2001, 2013, 2025	Snake
1966, 1978, 1990, 2002, 2014, 2026	Horse
1967, 1979, 1991, 2003, 2015, 2027	Goat (or Sheep)
1968, 1980, 1992, 2004, 2016, 2028	Monkey
1969, 1981, 1993, 2005, 2017, 2029	Rooster
1970, 1982, 1994, 2006, 2018, 2030	Dog
1971, 1983, 1995, 2007, 2019, 2031	Boar (or Pig)

You're Such an Animal!

Based on the above chart, you can review your animal-governed personality traits as predicted by this system.

Rat: The Rat is ever charming and aggressive, bearing a calm exterior that hides a restless soul. Rats love people and socialization, but are very selective with their friends. They keep problems to themselves, lacking true security, and always fear failure. However, the Rat is an amazing opportunist who has a great money-sensing tail. Their imagination, creativity, honesty, and good advice endear them to people easily. Good mates for the Rat are the Ox and Dragon. By the way, Shakespeare and Mozart were both born in the year of the Rat.

Ox: People born in the year of the Ox are quiet, patient, and methodical. This demeanor combined with contemplative idealism inspires confidence from others. Oxen must watch that their strong will and temper doesn't obstruct goals. They can become good leaders, being real workhorses and overly dutiful. The only trouble among Oxen is accepting new ideas. They're dogmatic and very slow to change, which makes them very devoted mates, but not romantic ones. In relationships, Ox fares best with Rats and Roosters. Among the Ox-born people we find Richard the Lionhearted and Aristotle.

Tiger: The Tiger is the proverbial "rebel with a cause," following that cause with reckless abandon just to test his limits. Tigers have a natural air of authority and if they take the time to look before they leap, they can be very successful. Typical Tigers are generous, sensitive, but not overly trusting. Good mates for Tiger include Horse, Dragon, and Dog. Some famous Tiger-born people are Mohammed and Marilyn Monroe.

Cat: Cat people are happy, refined, and virtuous (at least by appearance). Beneath all that you'll discover a feline filled with ambition, intelligence, and a highly social nature. They love to show off and entertain, but never really get intimate with anyone. Cat people are good with money, and keep their balance in difficult situations. Good mates for the Cat include Goat, Dog, and Boar. Famous Cats include Confucius and Henry Wadsworth Longfellow.

Dragon: Dragons are perhaps the most vital of all the animal signs, despite themselves. These direct, courageous, and stubborn individuals have no sense of tact, which either irritates others or inspires trust. They can be overly emotional, leaving logic behind in some matters, but they are also very intelligent, showing tremendous cleverness when focused on a task. In relationships, Dragon is a bit of a hermit, but does well when teamed up with Rat, Snake, or Rooster. Famous dragons include Sigmund Freud and Lewis Carroll.

Snake: People born during Snake's year exhibit great wisdom, goodwill, humor, and charm. They like to dress everything up and appeal to the public eye, including the presentation of their knowledge and ideals. Snakes follow through on their commitments, make firm decisions, and have luck with money. In love, they can be a bit jealous, making the Ox or Rooster the snake's best companion. Among Snake people we find Gandhi and Charles Darwin.

Horse: Horses are physically appealing people who love sports and socialization. They exhibit upbeat, humorous personalities and are always popular. The only real problem happens when Horse gets an ambition in his head. Then they can trample others in exuberance.

People governed by Horse energy have sound financial abilities, but aren't great advisors, especially in
matters of the heart. Good companions for the Horse
are Goats, Dogs, and Tigers. Famous Horse people
are Issac Newton and Charlemagne.

Goat: Goats are elegant and charming. They love Nature
and always seek after those sweet, greener grasses.
Goats graze slowly through life, often loosing track
of time or procrastinating so much as to become a
nuisance to others. Even so, the goat's manners make
up for his faults, and they absolutely adore anything
supernatural. The best mates for the Goat are Cat,
Pig, or Horse. Among the notable goats we find
Alexander Graham Bell and Mark Twain.

Monkey: Monkeys are full of mischief, playfulness, and energy
that desperately needs a focus. People born in the
Monkey's year have good memories, reasonable social skills, and astonishing inventiveness, all of which
are easily dissuaded by anything new or interesting.
Monkeys become dramatic, clever opportunists, especially toward things that feed the ego. To balance this energy, the best Monkey mates are Rat
and Dragon. Famous Monkies include Homer and
Susan B. Anthony.

Rooster: Roosters love flattery. These people crow loudly
about personal opinions to the point of aggressiveness. They are brutally honest, with no idea of how to
take a diplomatic tact. Roosters live a life of bold
adventure always building proverbial castles in the
sky, but rarely putting down foundations. The best
mates for Rooster are Ox, Snake, or Dragon. Famous Roosters include Maria de Medici and Rene
Descartes.

Dog: Dog people are worrisome, defensive, alert, intro-
verted, single-minded, and downright stubborn. They
are always intent on duty and detail to the point of
becoming their undoing. Dogs hate injustice to the
point of growling pessimistically about it, but they
balance this with unwavering loyalty, often making
sacrifices for those they love. Good mates for the Dog
include Horse, Tiger, and Cat. Famous Dogs include
Socrates and Louis XVI.

Boar: Boars are the most obliging and naïve of the animal
signs. They can easily be fooled by others, because
they tolerate everyone's faults to the extreme. Other
common Boar traits include sincerity, honesty, inner
strength, passivity, a hunger for knowledge, willful-
ness, and a sense of duty that comes close to that of
Dog. Cat is the best companion for the Boar, and famous Boars include Ernest Hemingway and Andrew
Jackson.

What Does the Year Hold?

We mentioned previously that as the animal years change,
the influence they exert on each of the signs also transforms.
So, if you know what animal year it is, you can also predict what
type of year you will have based on your birth sign as follows:

Year of the Rat

Rats have an amazing year (especially for a writer). The
Ox accumulates money during this year, at least some of which
she should save. Tigers find their lives at a standstill, while
Cat discovers a mislaid trust. For Dragon people, investments
and relationships thrive. Snake discovers plenty of activity to
the point of being overwhelmed. Horses have a bad business
year. Goats don't fare well financially, either. Monkeys have a
"golden touch" with everything to which they put their minds

and hands. Rooster may wish to take a risk, but would be well advised to wait. Dogs have a tedious year, while Boars experience success with money and love.

Year of the Ox

Rats will have to work diligently this year to keep safe what they gathered in the previous one. Oxen continue to reap the rewards from hard work in the year bearing their name. Tigers should take absolutely no risks; this is a bad cycle for them. Cats find the Ox energy enhances their ability to land on their feet no matter what. The Dragon grapples with an authority figure that causes problems, while the little dragon, Snake, has more work than they know how to handle. Horses will find they have a good year in business, but not with relationships. Both Goats and Dogs would rather this year never happen, while Monkey and Rooster are doing fairly well. Finally, Boar has to learn to adapt quickly and keep her temper under tight reins.

Year of the Tiger

Rats feel very insecure and anxious in a year with the big cat prowling, and Oxen aren't feeling much better. Tiger, of course, shines brightly in the limelight. Cats, who prefer a quieter pace then their large cousin, find themselves uneasy in the midst of such rapid changes. Dragons don't mind the hectic nature of this year. They focus on their goals and often accomplish one or more of them! The Snake finds this year tiresome, but educational. Horse takes advantage of transitional times, riding off on some new quest or task. The Goat gets lost in all this commotion, the Monkey sits back finding all the fuss vastly amusing, and Rooster just plain hates this whole year. The Dog displays devotion and finds happiness as a result, while Boar (as before) just adapts to the changes and keeps on "keep'n on."

Year of the Cat

If Rat felt uneasy last year, the situation certainly isn't improving. Rat needs to be very careful and watchful, especially toward Cat people with hidden agendas. Oxen find that things are getting a little bit better, and the Tiger rests blissfully on the laurels attained in the previous 12 months. Cat has no troubles in their own year, being able to enjoy both leisure and business at their own pace. Dragons enjoy the ambiance right now, and seem to shine more brightly, while Snake takes a much-needed breather, discovering some success afterward. For the Horse, this is a steady year for business and relationships, and Goat finally gets a little attention for her ongoing efforts. Monkeys experience a terrific professional year, and Roosters are still being quiet—recuperating from the previous woes. Dog rests contentedly, and Boar has a strong year in all areas of life except in legal matters.

Year of the Dragon

Rat experiences a generally pleasant year under Dragon's rule. Oxen have to be cautious to put down strong roots for anything new they undertake. Tiger loves Dragon's influence; it's a year of pomp and circumstance. Cats prefer to be homebodies and watch everyone else's activities. Dragons revel merrily in their own year, and the Snake finds true peace. The Horse will be satisfied with what life brings this year, and Goats and Monkeys should plan for 12 months of fun. Rooster could find the ideal mate or partnership situation this year, while Dog wants to retreat under a table and hide alone. Boars stay to their own kind, which is the safest place to be.

Year of the Snake

Rats would do well to take this year for contemplation or a personal hobby, and stay away from business altogether. Oxen may have trouble at home that requires cooling their easily heated temper. Tiger feels the need to get out, explore, and find some type of adventure. Cats experience a similarly good year, while Dragons continue to revel in the success from the previous 12 months. This is Snake's year, they can do anything!

Horse finds herself tempted to give up everything for a passion or love, but it would be a mistake to do so. For the Goat, it should be an interesting year (or at least not boring), and Monkeys receive all manner of unexpected opportunities. Roosters have problems in the roost, Dogs spend this entire year pondering and discovering new things, and Boar has a great business year but, sadly, will not find love.

Year of the Horse

Rat is going to have to apply all their financial fortitude toward juggling debts. Oxen seem to inherit Rat's more typical luck with business and have a strong financial year. Tigers start feeling restless, wanting to begin something new, and Cats simply have a very pleasant year filled with happiness. Dragons can be very successful under Horse's influence, some even moving into leadership positions. For the Snake, disappointment in love awaits, and the poor Horse can't find anything redeeming whatsoever about the year bearing her name. Goats have a lot of fun this year, while Monkeys seem distracted from play long enough to compete for good jobs. Roosters move smoothly ahead, Dogs are restless and irritated, and Boars get life back in order even though they're still experiencing troubles.

Year of the Goat

Rats begin to recoup their losses this year, while the tables turn on the Oxen and their debts rise. Tigers need to lie low because trouble waits. Cats experience some disappointments, and even Dragons may find they have difficulties if they get too involved in a relationship or project. It is Snake's year for romance this year (but it's slow in coming), while Horse has many improvements to look forward to. Goat finally discovers personal potential and applies it; Monkey plots and plans, but accomplishes little; and Rooster falls off the fence into all kinds of predicaments. Poor Dog is totally downhearted, but Boars are hopeful, seeing that both their personal and career goals are finally moving forward.

Year of the Monkey

Rats no longer chase their tails; life has finally returned to some form of symmetry and happiness. Oxen continue experiencing lousy luck. Tigers have a great deal of nervous energy and ideas, few of which are sound, and fewer still materialize. Cats pace themselves this year, and Dragon follows their example by staying uncharacteristically in the background of situations, not wishing to be tarnished by exposure. Snakes use wisdom and learn to cope in Monkey's year, while Horse displays surprising political savvy. Goat becomes a wallflower again, and Monkeys have the time of their lives through the whole 12 months. Rooster becomes moralistic and pompous, Dog rushes into situations where angels fear to tread, and the Boar has a fine year, especially with his or her mate.

Year of the Rooster

Rats continue with business success and can finally enjoy some fruits of those labors socially. Ox gets his or her life back on track, while the Tiger becomes the rebel (with, or without, a cause). Cats are discontent in the Rooster's year, but Dragons can shine if they remain cautious. Snakes have a difficult time, but Horses and Boars both achieve impressive success through hard work. Goat takes the year for personal recreation. Monkey no longer revels in her victories of the previous year, and may find they partied a little too hearty. The Rooster, of course, has everything well under control, while the Dog experiences disappointments from her previous haste.

Year of the Dog

Rat should return her focus wholly on business matters. Oxen have a gloomy year, while Tigers embark on great causes, being driven by wanderlust. Cats are uneasy and take precautions that may hold them back. Meanwhile, Dragons can achieve almost anything, and Snakes want to make changes but refuse to put energy toward those goals. Horses keep working for personal pleasure, Goats feel woefully neglected, and Monkeys bide their time until the financial constraints end. The Dog has a modestly good year, knowing that effort and service have their own rewards. Boars have a quiet year with steady financial flow.

Year of the Boar

This is a time for Rats to plan for the future and perhaps invest. Oxen come out of the dark times of the previous year, and Lady Luck visits Tigers in abundance. The Cat regains their sense of composure and contentment, Dragon's shrewdness provides financial gain, and Snake tries to simply roll with this year's punches. Horses have money in the Boar's year, and begin to realize their dreams. Goats and Monkeys both have profits coming. Conversely, Roosters work very hard for little gain. The Dog stays close to home, and rightfully so, while the Boar turns anything and everything into fortunes.

In terms of magick, it's a little more difficult to apply the Chinese animal signs to our spells and rituals because they span a year. Perhaps the best way of utilizing them is by being proactive. For example, because Monkey anticipates searching for work in the Year of the Horse, they could work job-oriented magick during that entire year, while Dogs might enact spells for inner peace, and Boars craft rituals to banish negativity.

Chapter 7

Feng Shui Bestiary

It is essential when learning something, you must study it in a holistic way. To be passionate about something means that you need to know its source and its application.

—Siou-Foon Lee

Feng shui is a philosophy that creates an environment which is ergonomic; it lets us work efficiently, comfortably and successfully by following the patterns of nature.

—Jenny Liu

Feng shui can be combined with animal magick in one of two ways. The first way is using feng shui to improve the quality of life for our animal companions. In this case the placement of food bins, beds, and other animal care products would be the keynote to our efforts. The second way would be to place images of various animals at specific points in and around our home to improve energy flow. This chapter discusses practical ways to broach both methods.

What we are presenting here is in part traditional feng shui, and in part a bit of personal adaptation. We feel that feng shui offers a completely functional means by which to bend and turn energy without upsetting the natural balance. In this, it blends beautifully with the ethics of the wild Witch. But there are only a few sources that discuss animal symbolism for traditional feng shui regions, and there is no means by which one could combine Western metaphysics with applied Eastern philosophy. So, in true pragmatic form, we took some artistic license here by gently (and respectfully) mixing the two systems into something that could augment the wild Witch's kit.

The Art of Placement

Before we can get into more "hands on" methods, one must first have a fairly good understanding of what feng shui is and how and why it's used. Feng shui originated in China about 4,000 years ago. Feng shui effectively combines ecology, geology, psychology, and ergonomics. The goal of this system is to inspire a positive flow of life energy (called chi) in our lives and living spaces. Chi is part of everything from the sand and stones to the stars above. As we become aware of the chi's movements, we can adjust our homes, offices, and even vehicles to be more attuned to it. This, in turn, improves the proverbial "good vibes" with which we have to work on a daily basis.

Feng shui is based on direction. Pay particular attention to the elements and keynotes of each direction as presented below. These will prove helpful in choosing and positioning animal images for magickal results and in working feng shui for your pets and familiars (see page 138).

The Feng Shui Circle

The Northern point of a plot of land, a home, or a room is the financial center. It's oriented with the Element of Water, and the colors of black and blue. This region influences how successful you are in your job, and how upbeat you feel about your chosen career path. It can also manifest in the type of job you choose. For example, if a hearth resides due north, you may find yourself desiring a career in firefighting or as a chimney sweep! The keynote for northern energy is nurturing.

Moving one notch clockwise, we come to the Northeast sector, governing learning and education. Its Element is Earth, and its primary colors brown and yellow. Keep this region of your living space orderly to likewise keep your thoughts in order. The keynote for the Northeast is growth.

The East is one of the four main quarters of feng shui. Its Element is Wood, and its colors are light blue and shoot green. The Eastern center's main influence is over matters of family and health, but it also manifests whenever one starts something new. When you're starting to feel sick, make sure this part of the house is clean! The keynote for the East is stimulation.

Next is the Southeast. Here we find the chi focused on prosperity, abundance, and creative ideas. Its Element is Wood and the color is dark green. If you want things to blossom in your life, or when you need to overcome a creative blockage, place flowering plants in this region, and keep the doors open to foster the chi. The keynote for the Southeast is consistency.

The Southern portion of the home governs how others perceive your efforts, and how much recognition you receive in life. Its Element is Fire and the colors are red and purple. Focus on this part of the home when you wish to develop honor, virtue, steadfastness, and grace under pressure. The keynote for the South is energy.

Continuing sunward we come to the Southwest sector. Tend this area well when you wish to foster positive relationships, good fortune, family unity, and overall harmony. The element for this region is Earth, and its colors are brown and yellow. The keynote for the Southwest is comfort.

West is the part of the feng shui circle that influences authority figures and children (including the figurative children we have in our pets and projects). Its Element is Metal, and its colors gold, silver, and white. The keynote for the West is serenity.

Finally, the Northwest is the region where networking comes into play, along with helpful people in and around our lives. If you find you have trouble giving or receiving, this is the area to examine. Its element is Metal, and the propitious colors here are white, silver, and gold. The keynote for the northwest is service.

Celestial Animals (As Above, So Below)

So where, exactly, do animals fit into the chi energy and feng shui as a system? In truth, animals are actually already part of the whole picture. Feng shui recognizes that migratory patterns and other seasonal movements represent part of the Universe's model. In short: Animals are already integrated into Nature's classroom, not just on the physical plane but also the celestial one. Chinese culture reflected the importance of animals to the "above-below" principle in both their religious practices and mythologies. For example, people held special rituals to honor the Bird Star, thought to be a messenger from God (heralding Spring), and it was customary to hunt both tigers and river turtles as a means of communicating with well-regarded ancestral spirits.

The animal portraits in the sky heralded important changes on the earth below. Feng shui observed these shifting patterns for guidance, especially the four key celestial animals: the Dragon, the Bird, the Turtle, and the Tiger. The Green Dragon appeared in the sky as a harbinger of Spring, the Red Bird flew overhead in Summer, the White Tiger crouched watchfully in the Fall, and the Black Turtle looked down from above in Winter. The colors and the timing of the animal's appearance correspond with the specific quarters on one's property and within the home.

Of the four animals, the Green Dragon is the most powerful and auspicious. The breath of the Dragon consists of positive chi, making this creature one of determination, courage, strength, and good fortune. Turtle is also quite important, because according to legend it was this creature who provided the magickal pattern for the Lo Shu square, the pattern on which the eight main segments of feng shui (and their influences on each other) are based, not to mention various Taoist principles.

Putting this all together on Earth meant that feng shui practitioners had to become astute observers of even subtle shifts in landscape. Land with Dragons (mountainous, hilly or undulating) is the most propitious land near which to build or live. Mind you, a hill that looks like a turtle's shell represents the Turtle, not the Dragon. A mountainous region with smaller hills nearby implies the presence of the White Tiger with the Dragon, working in harmony; whereas a similar formation before the Turtle's shell indicates the presence of the Red Bird. If that didn't sound complicated enough, there apparently are various types of dragons. Jagged mountains are Fire Dragons, while smooth ones are Water Dragons, squarish, flat-toped mountains are Earth Dragons, round hills are Metal Dragons, and steep climes are Wood dragons! However, we're pleased to report that you need not become a master of geography to utilize this art effectively.

Feng Shui Animals Outdoors

In this system, every home works best when surrounded by the four animal spirits placed in the same position or order as they turn in the seasonal array. The back, or South, of the house should be shielded by Turtle energy. If you have a hill or mountain behind you, that counts, otherwise you may wish to find the image of a turtle to place out back, with a mirror attached turned toward the home to redirect the chi. This is also the ideal location in which to enact spells and rituals for protective energy. You can call on Turtle as an ally in that effort.

The front, or North, of the house, specifically the doorway, should have Bird energy. That's why a home should always include an open area such as a courtyard to allow the Bird free-flying space. If you don't have this, an alternative is painting doors or stair railings red to honor the Bird's energies. This color also welcomes the appropriate type of chi into the home— the energy of Summer's abundance and prosperity. However, bird images (such as those on flags or wind chimes) can redirect energy, too. Another good item to put at the front of the home is the image of the beaconing cat known as *Maneki-Neki*, preferably near the doorway, for improved fortune and health. In any case, this is the best region of your home in which to work spells and rituals for hospitality, liberation, and prosperity.

To the East we seek out protection from the Dragon because this is the point of the rising sun and very potent yang energies. Consider enacting spells and rituals here aimed at hopefulness, mindfulness, and strengthening leadership abilities. If you have a tall building in the East, it represents the Dragon's height. Appropriate substitutions include having something green to the East or Dragon images.

To the West we seek out Tiger as this is the yin energy, neatly balancing the Dragon on the opposite side of creation. Good themes for spells and rituals in this region include improving psychic awareness, intuitiveness, and nurturing skills. If you have a shorter building on the West, it symbolizes the crouching Tiger. If not, use something white (a plant that blossoms with white flowers is ideal) or Tiger images to encourage this energy.

For readers with gardens, this whole concept presents a wonderful landscaping opportunity. Take a small dollhouse or other weatherproof piece that represents your home and put it in the middle of the garden. To the North of the house put the image of the Dragon, a Bird to the South (or a birdbath), a Dragon to the East, and a Tiger to the West. If you're growing flowers, plant them so their colors align with the four feng shui animals, making a living mandala around the item that symbolizes your home. From a purely magickal perspective, if you do this, you do not need to have the imagery around the exterior of the house. (Note: Feng shui experts would disagree, but this concept is based on Wild Witchery combined with the feng shui patterns.)

Those of you who rent rooms or apartments need not be discouraged. Use the same patterning within your personal space as close to the directional quarter and outer walls as possible. And if that's not feasible, try adding those animals to your protective visualizations. Imagine a glowing ball of chi energy all around your space with the four celestial creatures in their respective quarter, guarding that area diligently. Do, however, try to find some way to honor and thank those energies in your personal space (perhaps by wearing four charms, one for each creature, or getting small figurines that you keep on your altar in the appropriate directional quarter).

Feng Shui Animals Indoors

As we mentioned in the outdoor suggestions, one may certainly apply the celestial bestiary to the entirety of your indoor space, or any single room. However, don't stop there! Each feng shui region can be augmented symbolically by using animal imagery, too. How? Let's return to each segment and look at them separately:

North: When you find your finances are on iffy ground, or your career seems to be stagnating, try putting a live tank of fish here, particularly ones that bear black and blue colorations to get the chi flowing (and vital) again. Traditionally, this part of the house is supposed to face a mountain for protection. If it's not, put the image of a Dragon here.

Northeast: When you find your ability to concentrate goes awry, or you can't grasp a new subject effectively, place the image of a wise owl (preferably brown) in this region. An alternative here is the Antelope or Mouse for mental agility and attention to detail, respectively (note that these two creatures have stronger "earth" energies than the Owl).

East: Make adjustments in the East when you find your family quarreling, when you're feeling under the weather, or when you can't get a new project off the ground. For family oriented energies, turn to pack animals that have a sense of devotion, such as the Dog. For health, consider the Snake for transformation, or the frog, often used by Shamans in healing rituals. The images of these animals might be best carved in wood to honor this region's element.

Southeast: When either the richness of your ideas or your pockets seems wanting, this is the part of the home that needs your attention. Make sure there are no harsh corners or other items that "box in" the flow of chi. Consider adding the image of a beaver to this region, as this creature symbolizes sensible resourcefulness in any area of your life. An alternative that focuses more on prosperity would be a wooden image of the Buffalo, who encourages improvements that come by your own good efforts.

South: If people are gossiping about you, or it seems that no matter what you do your efforts are misinterpreted, adjust this portion of your living space. Put a seven-day red candle in this region adjacent to the image of a Dragonfly, who bears the medicine of wise communication in his wings. Alternatively, look to a pathfinder such as the Wolf, who can guide you through the underbrush of misunderstanding.

Southwest: When those with whom you live are constantly bickering or restless, this is the region in which the chi has been disrupted. Choices of animal imagery here include a Beaver, who teaches effective teamwork; Swallow, who reminds us of the sanctity of our homes and the power of perspective; or the Prairie Dog, who stresses community energy. If you can combine this imagery with a potted plant in order to reflect the Earth-oriented nature of this region, all the better.

West: If an authority figure seems to be bullying you, or the children in and around your life are showing signs of illness, strife, or rebellion, those issues begin here. For those without children, consider the figurative children in your life, such as pets and special projects to which you devote tremendous attention. For imagery, look to the Cowbird, who governs parent-child relationships; Bear to improve personal convictions and inner fortitude; Skunk for the power of self-assertion; or Butterfly for positive transformations. Whatever your choice, look for a representation in metal that's gold or silver-toned to honor this sector's colors and element.

Northwest: When you're having trouble making the connections you need, when there doesn't seem to be anyone to help you with pressing matters, or you find your ability to give to others wanting, check this area for blockages. Bring metallic images of Spider spirit to help you weave your web of friends and acquaintances more effectively, Pelican for selflessness, or Turkey to learn the lesson of the "give away."

There are also some "luck" animals according to various feng shui traditions that you can consider in this mix as well. These include:

Bat:	Good health.
Bird Pairs:	Luck in relationships.
Carp:	Enhanced studies, business success.
Cat:	Luck.
Cicada:	Fertility.
Cow:	Wish fulfillment.
Crane:	Longevity.
Dog:	Loyalty.
Double fish:	Ward off evil.
Dragon and tortoise:	Long-lasting success, courage and determination.
Dragon with pearl:	Potentialities.
Duck:	Romantic devotion and bliss in relationships.
Eight horses:	Strength and perseverance.
Eight turtles:	Long life and success.
Elephant:	Lifting burdens.
Fish:	Luck and wealth.
Foo dog:	Protection.
Four monkeys:	Virtue.
Galloping Horse:	Honor and rewards, tenacity.
Lion:	Safety, valor, and wisdom.
Mouse:	Money and abundance.

Ox:	Industry.
Panda:	Joy.
Phoenix and dragon:	Honor, power, and righteousness.
Pig with piglets:	Prosperity.
Rabbit:	Honesty, sensitivity.
Rat:	Attention to detail, order.
Rooster:	Charm and courage.
Sheep:	Generosity.
Snake:	Recovery and peace.
Striding Horse:	Confidence and diligence.
Three monkeys:	Sagacity.
Three rams:	Auspicious energies.
Tiger:	Strength, power, protection.
Tortoise:	Success in business, endurance.
Unicorn:	Fosters longevity.

If you think you've noticed some similarities here with the 12 signs of the Chinese Animal Zodiac, you're right! There are quite a few crossovers. Feng shui applied the predominant characteristics of the Zodiac creatures to this art for more finely tuned, personalized results.

You don't have to wait until there's a problem evidencing to bring animal energies into any part of your home. For example, if you're working spells and rituals to simply maintain the quality of family communications, you could also consider enacting those activities in the appropriate feng shui region, integrating suitable animal symbolism. This way, you encourage a positive flow of chi and magick all at the same time.

For individuals with very little personal space within which they can easily make these kinds of changes, may we suggest setting up your altar (or even the top of a bookcase) so that it reflects the eight feng shui sections. As you need specific energies, place animal figurines, colors, elements, and/or pictures in the appropriate segment(s) on the surface. Leave these items in place until the desired shift manifests. Make sure to keep both the objects and this surface clean and free of clutter. Dust and nonfocused items disrupt the flow of chi.

Please remember that what we are presenting here is an intuitive interpretation of feng shui as it could potentially combine with animal magick in your living and working environments. These are examples only. Don't be afraid to refer to the totemic association in Appendix B, or other books about animal symbolism or feng shui so you can personalize and adapt these ideas more suitably to your path and vision.

Feng Shui for Pets and Familiars

Feng shui experts tell us that having healthy, loving animals in our homes is very good for the overall flow of chi. For example, having fish, especially in the Northern part of a home or business, encourages flowing finances and overall success. This concept comes as no great surprise to wild Witches, who tend to have more than one pet, and at least one familiar. Animals provide comfort, companionship, diversion, and some, such as dogs, also protect. Now it's our turn to return the gifts so generously provided by our pets.

In Nature, animals live harmoniously with the energies that surround them. When animals spend most or all of their time in artificial indoor environments, they are at the mercy of whatever energies we create. And just as with humans, these energies can greatly affect their health and emotional well-being. And even a home that's been carefully designed by feng shui guidelines for humans may not be harmonious for your animal companions.

Try to look at the world from your pet's perspective. How cluttered are their living spaces? How open? What is their day-to-day reality like? When you begin to see the world from a dog or cat's view you can also begin to adjust the chi of your home for that creature's benefit. In many ways, this is akin to making sacred space, only directed toward the benefit of your pets.

The Western region governs the proverbial children of your home, so take a very close look at this region. Remove any clutter or debris from any entrance or walkway here. This will ensure that chi is welcoming and inviting. Make sure that there is nothing obstructing any doorways and that the door(s) can open fully. This will ensure that all of the chi can enter and thereby fill the space with all the best energies for your pet.

Other helpful hints for using feng shui to benefit your pets include:

- Never place the animal's bed, tank, or cage under a window. This invites the chi to escape while the creature sleeps, and chi is best kept circulating through the house rather than rushing in and out of the window.

- Don't place your pet's bed between two doors. Bad sha (a hard, harsh energy) might rush in one, envelop the animal, and then rush out the other.

- Never allow your pets bed to be next to a bathroom wall nor directly below a toilet. Bad yin energy from the toilet can cause loss of health.

- Don't place your pet's bed in a direct line with the door. All the animal's chi and good luck will drain out through the door, along with the creature's favorite toys and any hidden treats.

- If you must put the pet's bed or bowls in long hallways or entryways, hang a half moon and sun image above the area. This disperses any hard energy (sha).

🗶 Look for obviously protruding corners and edges in the creature's favorite spaces. These edges cut into the electromagnetic field, causing a loss of energy (mind you, for over-active puppies and kittens, you might want to *add* a few corners).

🗶 Give your pet a red collar, pillow, or decorative item for their sleeping space. Red is the most fortunate, positive color in feng shui, encouraging health and happiness.

🗶 If you're worried about your pet wandering, add a few heavy stones into their living environment. These encourage stability.

🗶 In determining the placement for your pet's sleeping area, watch to see the area to which they're drawn naturally again and again. Dogs in particular will sleep in the area of the home with good feng shui.

🗶 When training your pet, work in the Northeast portion of your home for best results.

🗶 When your pet is ailing, move their bed or food dish to the Eastern sector to encourage improvements, and check this region for neatness and clarity.

🗶 If your pet seems restless, spend quiet time with him in the Southwest region of your home to reestablish tranquility.

🗶 Hang a cut crystal in a window where the light will shine on your pet regularly, improving the flow of chi toward them.

🗶 If you have an uncoordinated pet, put the image of a three-legged toad near its sleeping space. This is a feng shui symbol for improved luck.

Outcomes and Expectations

What can you anticipate from blending wild Witchery with feng shui? Mostly slow and steady improvements. While our magick can increase the manifestation pace and power of this system somewhat, feng shui is considered a gentle art. This is based on the idea that lasting change takes time. At least part of the positive change that happens here is simply on the level of our awareness. When we make ourselves alert to the energies around us, we can then work with them more effectively toward happier, healthier lives. In other words, you will adjust your internal landscape to accept positive chi, just as you adjusted your environment to produce it!

Chapter 8

Totems, Guides, Familiars, and Teachers

The ancient Egyptians, Africans, and Native Americans all respected and even worshiped animals. Believed to possess all manner of virtues, animals were frequently eaten or sacrificed to release their positive attributes. Perhaps this sounds rather gruesome to modern-minded folk, but our ancestors were not doing this without thought, and without honoring the animal's spirit in every way possible. Consider for a moment that the word *animal* comes from the Latin *anima*, meaning breath of life, or soul. By extension, this implies that humans felt that animals had spirits, so such offerings were not taken lightly.

In addition to offerings, we see some of the Shamanic respect toward animals through various hunting traditions. The medicine people of a tribe would sometimes seek out a specific animal ritualistically, then use that creature's parts in cloaks, necklaces, masks, etc. While this might seem like an odd way to honor a totem animal, it was truly a kind of communion. To hunt the animal, the person had to think like the creature, move through its habitat, apply aromas that would blend into that setting, and reconnect with the wild within. After the hunt, the animal's spiritual aptitudes became part of the Shaman's kit, and the creature's various parts represented that partnership and power.

While such sacrifices and rituals are infrequent in Neo-Pagan traditions today, we remain aware of this history and the reverence toward animals. Before proceeding further into how we honor this tradition, let's define terms as they are used in this chapter:

Totem: A totem can be seen as the spiritual embodiment of all natural creatures of that type. Typically, totems are life-long associates and spiritual partners. Note that totems can be personal or group oriented.

Familiar: A living creature that bonds with a Witch or magickal practitioner and becomes a spiritual partner. In ancient times it was believed that if one's familiar died, you did, too.

Power Animal: The spiritual embodiment of a creature on which one can call for assistance in other world journeys, in applying specific attributes that come from that creature, and in other magickal processes. During other world journeys, the power animal protects and guides the practitioner. Power animals can work alone or in tandem, and the medicine of these creatures can be temporary or lifelong.

Animal Guide: Another spiritual embodiment of a creature that comes bearing a lesson, aid, or a message for a practitioner. Animal guides are typically temporary (they come when needed, and leave when the situation resolves itself).

Animal Medicine: The term *medicine* refers to the special powers housed in each part of creation, including the animal kingdom. By observing animals in natural surroundings and their associated behaviors, we begin to get glimpses of each creature's medicine. This understanding, in turn, helps us connect with the animal spirit, honor it, and utilize it in our wild Witchery.

We've mentioned previously in this book that we feel it's important to get to know the natural animal before attempting to contact and work with the supernatural energies of any creature. At this point, however, a few of you are likely thinking, *where am I going to find all these wild creatures if I live in an apartment in the middle of a city?* This is a very important question and one that should be examined before we discuss magickal processes for discerning and communing with totems any further.

One thing to bear in mind is that your awareness of a natural creature can certainly be improved by remote studies. There are dozens of books, sites on the Internet, pictures and sculptures, and so on of animals that you can find in the library, on your computer, or at art galleries. While this isn't quite as intimate as being "up close and personal" with a creature, if it is the only option you have, use it!

Alternately, our suggestion to our urbanite readers would be to check with your local visitor's center and find out the locations of nearby city, state, or national wildlife refuges, forests, or parks. Zoos are also an option (but remember, the animals won't exhibit natural behaviors because of the man-made habitat). There's bound to be one of these options within a reasonable commuting distance from where you live. The effort you make to visit one of these places will be well worth your time. Remember, however, that if you are not experienced with back-country hiking or the proper use of a compass, stick to well-marked trails and always tell someone at home where you are going and when you expect to return. It's also a good idea to check in with ranger stations and advise them where you can be found if you fail to return by your appointed time, or if inclement weather threatens.

We should mention again at this juncture that other than observing animals from a safe distance, you should never try to actually interact with a wild animal, totem or not. The most obvious reason is the threat of disease, which can work both ways: Wild animals can transmit diseases to humans and domestic livestock, and visa versa. The next obvious reason would be the physical threat the animal could pose to you in the event of an attack. The less obvious reason is the threat you pose to the animal. Wild animals view anything out of the ordinary (such as a human stomping through the woods) as a potential threat, and any threat causes an animal stress. Stressed animals will disrupt their feeding patterns, waste precious calories in evasive maneuvers, interrupt courtship and mating behaviors, abandon their young, and in some extreme cases, even abort early stage fetuses. Stressed animals are also prone to attacking whatever it is that they perceive as a threat and a stressed animal does not necessarily react in a predictable fashion.

If you want to interact with an animal, then do so with respect. Respect their boundaries and their natural behaviors, don't try to impose your perceptions on them. Enter their natural habitats quietly and leave the same way. Invest in a good brand of binoculars. Buy a spotting scope. Take your camera or video recorder along. See with your eyes...hear with your ears...smell with your nose...but only touch with your heart.

Mythical Totems or Spirit Guides?

Some of the more interesting and beautiful early books were called bestiaries. These clever tomes often featured highly illuminated text with myths and descriptions of fabled beasts from around the world. These creatures varied greatly—from the Basilisk, Gryphon, Unicorn, and Salmander to Hippogriffs, Dragons, and Sea Monsters. While these animals are not part of the natural world as we know it, they have features from many natural animals. This begs the question: Can one have a Mermaid or Pegasus (or whatever) as a totem or spirit guide?

This is not an easy question to tackle. The power of myth is not something to simply shrug off as meaningless to our pursuits of animal magick. The legends and lore of animals evidence themselves in the symbolism and attributes we give these spirits. Additionally, in theory, it is possible for something that's held in the communal mind for a long time to develop as a viable thought form with all the energies and attributes given it by that collective. So if you happen to believe in unicorns and other amazing creaturesas totems or guides, there is some theory to substantiate your beliefs.

There are also cultures that associate with a mythological animal. For example, in China, the dragon might be considered a cultural totem for the entire nation. Nonetheless, there does not seem to be a historical precedence for individuals having these creatures as a companion or guide.

Having said that, it may be possible to have such a creature as a totem or spirit guide, but it is nowhere near as probable as a natural animal spirit. Should such an arceytpal thought form come to you in meditations or dreams, consider its symbolic values before jumping to the conclusion that this is indeed a power animal or other similar manifestation. Stretching your imagination is a good thing, as is keeping an open mind, but discovering a totem isn't about what's cool or hip, or seemingly powerful. It represents something of yourself, of your spiritual path, and it should always be treated with respect, be it the simple earthworm or the grandest dragon.

Recognizing Animal Spirit Guides and Totems

Before you can adequately work with animal spirit guides and totems, you must first discern which ones are truly yours. One of the most important things in this whole discovery process is to put aside expectations from the start. If you go searching for a totem thinking that you must have an Eagle (as an example), you will close the doors to other animal helpers by having preconceptions. You might very well have Eagle in your future, but if you never allow all of Nature's spirits to speak to you as they choose, you will never know for sure.

Another thing to bear in mind with expectations is that typically a person, group, or nation only has *one* totem animal. All others are guides and guardians. Don't automatically assume that the first time you try to connect with an animal spirit that whatever you encounter is necessarily your totem. That is simply not the case.

With those caveats out of the way, there are several ways in which you can determine your totem animal(s). For one, a simple, unexplainable prevalence of a creature in your life is a clue. If something keeps appearing in the oddest places, ask yourself why. Better still, ask the creature! At some point or another you will have to get past the letters of introduction and figure out why this being has come into your life, and sometimes all it takes is a simple query.

Communing With Animal Spirits

So, how do you go about asking? Prayer, meditation, and dream work are three options. Of these three, prayer is perhaps the simplest approach. Entreat the animal spirit to reveal itself to you somehow and explain its presence. If the creature responds, it likely will be through one of your senses or with empathy (this is often true in meditation). For example, say you notice that crane images were appearing everywhere around you—on billboards, on business cards, in TV commercials, etc.

This would be a good time to seek out Crane and ask why. If you feel cold after your entreaty, the interpretation might be that you've become so fiercely independent and distanced yourself from intimacy so much that you have cut out any warmth in your life.

A second alternative is meditation. Simply close your eyes and breathe, mentally calling for a totem or guide to come to you. There is no predicting how long this might take. Set yourself up for a specific amount of time and wait. If nothing happens on the first try, keep trying! Nature has Her own sense of what constitutes the "right" time to reveal such things, and usually it's not in keeping with a human "ideal." In reading over various people's experiences, the revelations often come in the last moments of trying, almost as if to test our resolve. Who says Nature spirits don't have a sense of humor?

A third way of seeking animal spirits is in the dream world (see page 65). You can preface your sleep time with specific metaphysical aids such as prayer, chanting, and meditation to help open the spiritual doorways to your subconscious and gently usher in a sleep-trance state. Additionally, you might wish to place a dream catcher over your bed, burn incense that promotes dreaming (such as rose, jasmine, lotus, sandalwood, and marigold), play some type of soundtrack that features Nature's orchestra (rain, crickets, etc.), and put some type of welcoming items on your altar (such as a book of animal imagery).

While it may take some time and practice to communicate effectively with spirits in dreamtime, if one comes to you make sure to ask the questions you had in your heart. Make sure to have some means of recording your dreams when you wake so you can record any fleeting images, feelings, or messages that an animal spirit brings.

As far as interpreting the animal spirit's meanings in any of these scenarios, that depends a lot on what shows up and how the creature communicates. Some will be very literal, others symbolic, and other's still will reflect the creature's personality traits. Bull, for example, is not known for being delicate or beating around the bush; Alligator might get snappy; Butterfly might speak in imagery; and Squirrel's message might be prudently short. That's why we always recommend making notes or taping insights about your encounter afterward. Beyond the meaning becoming clearer over time, some missives will have to do with things that have yet to manifest, or things that you can only comprehend with the help of time's hands.

Totem Medicines

The following is a quick reference list of common totem animals, and their key medicine and attributes. For more details, refer to Appendix B.

Alligator: Adaptation; survival.

Ant: Tenacity; discipline; and teamwork.

Bat: Cleansing; guide of the night.

Bear: Healing; nurturing; rejuvenation; empathy; goals.

Beaver: Building; gathering; teamwork.

Buffalo: Providence; health; prayerfulness.

Butterfly: Transformation; liberation; good choices.

Cougar: Bravery; fast action; balance.

Coyote: Playfulness; humor.

Crane: Independence; solitude.

Crow: Universal law.

Deer: Gentle kindness; sensitivity; support; serenity.

Dolphin: Breath; life force.

Dragonfly: Activity; change (often improvements).

Eagle: Warrior energy; clear vision.

Elk: Power; strength; nobility; endurance.

Fox: Cunning; the conscious mind; adaptation.

Frog: Water energy; healing.

Hawk: Perspective; observation; spiritual awareness.

Horse: Movement; dependability.

Hummingbird: Messages; positive outlooks.

Lizard: Dreaming; frugality.

Lion: Voice; walking the walk.

Moose: Longevity; trustworthiness.

Mouse: Detail orientation.

Otter: Curiosity; empathy; leisure.

Owl: Sagacity; truth; psychism; insight.

Porcupine: Trust; self-images.

Rabbit: Fertility; alertness.

Raven: Change; shapeshifting; manifestation.

Salmon: Instinct; fortitude.

Seahorse: Poise; self-confidence.

Skunk: Self-assertion; actualization.

Snake: Transformation; rebirth.

Spider: Communications; networks; creativity; alternatives.

Squirrel: Energy; wise prudence; planning.

Swan: Symmetry; child-like outlooks; intuitiveness.

Turtle: Inventiveness within; decision-making; protection.

Whale: Sacred song.

Wolf: Loyalty; stability; forethought; tribal reconnection.

Connecting With Power Animals

You have finally found out that Bear is your totem. Now
what? How on earth do you begin connecting with these powers
both substantively and spiritually? That isn't an easy question
to answer, and we can't begin to cover all the potential totems
in one chapter, but we can give you some examples to ponder
or try in your explorations:

Bears

Bear is among the oldest of sacred animals, and its importance as such spanned the globe from Japan to Iceland. Native
Americans place Bear as the guardian of the West and believe
that bears and humans are related (because bears can stand
upright and even walk in that position for short distances). Siberian Shamans honor Bear as an ancestor and King of the
Forest, and in Crete Ursa Major and Minor are credited for
protecting Zeus from Cronos.

Many folks are attracted to the notion of having Bear as a
totem. Obviously, going into the wild in an attempt to observe
bears is not feasible for most in the best of circumstances, and
downright dangerous in the worst-case scenario. There is no
such thing as a "safe" wild bear! So what suggestions can I give
to those who feel that Bear is their totem? Read about them.
There are many books available, ranging from the strictly bio-
logical, to the myths and legends that surround this species.
Go to the zoo or a wildlife park. If you keep in mind that wild
animals behave differently in captivity, you can still learn a
great deal about a species simply by observing it. Meditate on
Bear and ask it to show you its secrets (try eating fish before-
hand, work in the Western quarter of your sacred space, or
put a piece on your altar as a gift to Bear). But above all, give
this animal a great deal of respect, and approach it cautiously—
even in spirit form!

Bee

Of all insects, bees received the most admiration and symbolic associations around the world. In Egypt, Ra weeps worker bees (giving them the symbol of industry and solar energy). In India, the byproduct of bees (honey) is often used in describing Vishnu; Aristotle regarded them as having divine attributes; and many peoples regarded their flight as a means of communicating with the heavens.

To connect with Bee, begin by watching one outdoors if you can. If you have a natural place where you can surround yourself with aromatic flowers, all the better (but observing from indoors will still work). Consider having a bit of honey on your altar (a comb if you can find one), a bit of sweet nectar, or mead (which is a honey wine). Also drink some tea with honey to internalize the Bee's vibrations.

As you meditate, begin humming softly. Keep it monotone, akin to buzzing. Again, the idea here is to align your aura with the Bee's energy. Wait and see what happens!

Bird

It is nearly universal that the flight of birds symbolizes the movement of spirit, the soul, and communications between humans and the Divine. Euripides called birds "heralds of the Gods" and birds are often to thank for heroes and prophets alike getting the information they need from heaven (thus the phrase "a little bird told me").

To connect with Bird, go to a place where you can be up high (get a "bird's eye" view), and if it's a windy location, all the better. Wear something light and airy. As you meditate, put your arms out as if to soar freely. Feel the winds just as a bird might sense it ruffling its feathers. Whistle with gladness for that liberation, then see if Bird joins you in your astral flight.

Canines

If you've a mind to connect on a spiritual level with the canine species, the opportunities are certainly available, though contact with the wild canine is discouraged! If you own a dog, or know someone who does, simply observing how it interacts with its human pack, other canines, other animal species, or human strangers can enhance your understanding of this species.

Begin by paying attention to how domesticated canines react to their environment. In particular, watch the position of the tail, the position of the mouth, and eye contact. A closed mouth with direct eye contact indicates tension of some type; an open mouth with indirect eye contact is more relaxed. Head lowered, front legs extended, hindquarters raised, and tail high is known as "play-bowing" and is an invitation to have some fun! A frontal stance is more aggressive than an off-centered stance, and any position where the belly is exposed is a yielding sign of trust. This information is similarly helpful should you encounter an unfamiliar dog or wild canine, such as a wolf.

By the way, you may mimic these body postures to invite or avert canine behaviors. To illustrate, a full frontal upright posture with direct eye contact will say, "I'm the Alpha here—don't mess with me!" while squatting with your body off-centered and indirect eye contact says, "I'm not here as a threat, and would like to make contact with you." Of course, you must be prepared for the consequences should a dog (or other canine species) choose to accept your challenge or reject your offers of friendship!

If you happen to be allergic to dogs, or are unable to interact or observe as described here, try squatting or standing on all fours in an off-centered position while meditating. This is a welcoming dog stance. Also consider having a bone or bit of fresh meat on your altar to honor Dog spirit.

Deer

Those who are seeking a connection with a deer species totem might want to spend some time in the forest, particularly along the edges where the woods border a field. This meeting of two different habitats is called an "edge-effect," and many animals make use of these areas. Walk slowly, stopping often to look and listen carefully. Deer rely heavily on their sense of hearing.

Remember that you are trying to establish connection with a prey-species, so you should be alert to your surroundings. When deer sense danger, they freeze in place; if the threat is real, they explode into action. If there is no threat they may continue to browse or may move silently away.

I've always accused deer of being able to become invisible; one minute you can clearly see them and the next minute they disappear. The secret is to move directly away from the viewer, using objects (such as trees or bushes) to break up your outline and not make any excess motions, because predators are alerted by movement. Watch where you place your feet; avoid stepping on sticks that may crack or dry leaves that may rustle, giving away your location.

If you cannot go to a location such as the one described, stand quietly, meditating, perhaps while some woodsy incense surrounds you. Imagine a rack of antlers on your head (ladies, you can do this, too—both sexes of caribou and reindeer have antlers). Feel the weight and balance of those antlers. Tilt your head back and take a deep breath through your nose, flaring your nostrils. Pay attention to what you see, hear, and smell; how the sun feels on your skin; and how the breeze moves through your hair (deer have hair, just as humans do, though deer hair is hollow, for insulation). Close your eyes. Can you pinpoint the direction of the sounds around you? Welcome to a deer's world!

Felines

It goes without saying that trying to connect with any member of the wild cat species would be a potentially fatal mistake! As with the Bear, contact with nondomesticated felines is best reserved for those moments at the zoo. Instead, we suggest sticking with first-hand interactions with house cats, which are still small versions of their larger family members.

Bearing in mind that most cat species prefer to hunt at night, and that they are adept at stalking their prey, those who are interested in Cat totems might want to spend some time learning to walk silently in the dark. People with Cat totems often have excellent night-sight, and may actually prefer the absence of bright light. Cats also have extraordinarily fast reflexes, so developing and honing hand-eye coordination would be advantageous. I don't advise trying to mimic a cat's jumping or climbing abilities, but martial arts would be an ideal form of athletic exercise for Cat people.

Should you be allergic to cats or not have the chance to interact with domestic ones, you can put a bit of cat food, cat nip, cream, fish, and/or a toy on your altar to attract Feline energies. Sit in a lazy sun puddle as you meditate, and drink some catnip tea. Pat at a feather or other feline toy, and see if Cat jumps in to play along.

Fish

Fish are among the most widely seen ancient symbols, having a variety of meanings. Frequently used as both food and offerings at rites for Ishtar and Venus; in Buddhism fish have associations with sacred law; and in Hindu mythology we read that Vishnu incarnated as a fish. Celts focus on salmon and trout as being representative of wisdom, foresight, and healing (specifically the healing water from sacred wells). And among many coastal people, this creature represents fertility and wealth.

Aquariums of any kind are an excellent place to observe fish in their environment. Get a feel for how they move and interact with each other and outside stimulus. In your meditations you could try being partially submerged in water (make sure you can't fall asleep accidentally). Eat some vegetable sushi for a taste of the sea (this is wrapped in kelp), listen to the sound of waves, and swim out through the astral to meet your guides.

Horses

Other than canines, horses have been the closest domesticated animal to humans for both pleasure and work. Horses were domesticated as early as 1750 B.C.E., and its symbolism reflects this ancientness. Hindus identify the horse with our physical body, which houses the spirit. In China a white horse is an avatar of Kwan yin, and in European tradition horses are regarded as prophetic, psychic, magickal, and an omen of prosperity.

The horse is a magnificent creature. In order to connect with Horse, we recommend that you go to a wide-open field and run. Run in a circle, run down a hill—just run! Feel the wind streaming through your mane. Feel your feet/hooves pounding on the earth. Feel your heart thundering in your chest. Feel the power of muscle and bone working in concert. Feel the spirit of freedom, for that is what Horse represents: power and freedom.

Lizard

In both Egyptian and Greek mythology, the lizard was an emblem of wisdom and luck. In Roman stories, a lizard sometimes took the place of snakes as either guardians or powerful spirits, the jinn. And among Native Americans, Lizard is a totem animal that bears the medicine of dreaming.

Lizards are creatures that enjoy humidity and heat. To connect with that spirit, lie on a large warm rock on a sunny day and sprinkle yourself periodically with water. If possible, bring some crickets or mealworms as a gift for Lizard and release them to the earth. If you're feeling really adventurous you could try some chocolate covered crickets yourself to internalize one of Lizard's favorite foods. As you meditate, visualize yourself in an arid location and keep your eyes open. Lizard doesn't often move quickly, unless hunting, so be patient.

Pigs

Pigs typically bear the symbolic value of prosperity and fertility. In its fertile aspect, it correlates with the Great Mother Goddess, and thus, has strong lunar overtones. In Celtic tradition in particular the domestic pig and wild boar played important roles, as the meat of this creature fed the gods.

For those who wish to commune with the Wild Pig or Boar totem, our first words of advice would be: *Do not try to commune in the same space as the wild species!* Until you have a complete understanding of each species' behaviors, do not endanger your life, or the life of the animal, by trying to force an encounter.

Your search for Boar will take you into the hardwood forests. Boar's sense of smell is far superior to its eyesight or hearing, so if you really want experience Boar, get on your knees, dig down into the soil with your hands, put your face close to the earth, and inhale (try not to snort any bugs in the process). Each soil type has a distinctive odor that is influenced by mineral content and the vegetation that grows from it and decays into it. What can you tell about the types of plants that are growing around you from what you smell in the soil? What minerals can you detect?

Boar is a patient animal, rooting slowly along the ground, exploring hollows under tree roots and searching for tasty grubs under rotting logs. Take your time and practice that patience. Just remember to wash your hands with soap after touching any unknown plant material before you touch your mucus membranes—eyes, nose, mouth, genitals—the last thing you want is a case of poison oak on your lips.

Boar is a fighter, so you might want to view your location from a defensive and offensive standpoint. What natural features surrounding you could offer you protection from an attack? If you were attacked, how would you fight back? Boar's natural defense is a thick, bristly hide that covers a body well protected in layers of fat. His greatest offense is his tusks, which he gnashes together, creating a menacing clicking sound that warns of his increasing agitation. Boar is a formidable enemy and it is of little wonder that warriors often associated with him and endeavored to emulate his courage and ferocity when they went to battle.

Turtle

As a water creature, the Turtle has strong associations with fertility, creativity, persistence, longevity, and the passing of time. In Hindu stories, the world rests on the back of a turtle, and the Vedas speak of a great Turtle who is called Lord of the Creatures. Japanese myths recount a tortoise as being a servant to the sea god, and also as a messenger between the worlds.

To connect with Turtle, get a large box and make holes in it for your head, arms, and legs (effectively creating a shell for yourself). Drink a small glass of water before your meditation to internalize that element, which is one that Turtle enjoys. Pull yourself into the shell. Feel the safety and quiet of that space. Call for Turtle to join you and commune in that sacred womb.

Present and Future Fauna

Many people ask if power animals, guides, and totems can change. Our feeling is that they can, and certainly do, change. Some animals stay with us for a season to teach a lesson, to strengthen, to assure, or provide insight. Others are so much a part of our makeup as to be with us a lifetime.

Who we are and what we need spiritually can change from moment to moment, let alone year to year. So why would our animal companions not shift to reflect those transformations? While totems tend to be lifelong, it's quite feasible that dramatic life alterations could lead to similar dramatic totemic shifts. It makes sense considering that this spiritual creature somehow reflects our very soul.

As you explore your guides and totems, and build relationships with them, keep this in mind. Just as you would not try to "possess" a friend, you cannot possess a spirit animal. It is wild and free, and comes to you as a gift. Accept it, treat it like the treasure it is, and honor it always.

In Closing

We hope that reading this book has awakened the wild Witch within you, or minimally made you more aware of the role of animal magick in modern Neo-Pagan traditions. We cannot say that this Path is right for everyone any more so than Druidism, Shamanism, Wicca, or any other New Age tradition can. What we can tell you is that working in Nature's classroom and diligently studying Her lessons is well worth any spiritual seeker's time. Nature bears the fingerprint of Universal Order and reflects the Divine in a unique and beautiful way. No matter your spiritual focus, glimpsing that pattern and appreciating it provides access to a whole other reality that is not temporal. Through it we can begin to see and comprehend our very souls.

Whatever your choice of Path, now, or in the future, we pray this book has given you that initial glimpse of the delicate balance between Nature, the wild within, and the enlightened being each of us can become.

Fair Winds and Sweet Water

Trish and Rowan

Parts is Parts:
Wildlife Laws and
Preservation Issues

Our ancestors commonly collected animal parts (bones, feathers, fur) for spiritual and magickal purposes. Possession of these parts was often believed to imbue the possessor with the attributes of the animal. Modern Pagan practitioners have rediscovered the power inherent in the plants and animals that share this planet with us, and many wish to connect with these powers by utilizing plant and animal parts. But here's the catch! Most wild animals (as well as wild plants) are protected in some way and there are state and Federal laws that regulate the possession, distribution, sale, and trade of wildlife parts. The honorable Pagan knows and accepts that, overall, these laws are in the best interest of Nature, and is willing to work within the confines of the laws.

So how does one go about being a law-abiding wild Witch or Shaman? A suggestion is to locate the phone number of your local state game and fish office (usually located under "State Government" in the phonebook), and give them a call. Ask for a copy of their state protected wildlife (and plants, if you plan on harvesting any wild plants) list and also request a copy of the statute that pertains to the possession and commerce of game species. This is important for each different state, because laws differ from place to place. For example, in Georgia, it's legal to harvest black bear during the state hunting season, but taking one in Mississippi is highly illegal because there they are protected as a threatened species. In Alaska it's legal to sell moose antlers, but only if the antlers are removed from the skull plate. Products made from deer antlers are legal to sell in some states, but are illegal in other states. Items made from domestic pheasant feathers are legal in most states to sell, but it is illegal anywhere in the U.S. to even have feathers from any bird protected by the Migratory Bird Treaty Act (most song-birds fall into this category). It pays to know the laws of the specific area in which they live.

People in general, and Americans specifically, have long held a love affair with the wildlife we cohabitate with on this planet. As early hunter-gatherers, we depended on wildlife to sustain us, clothe us, and to provide our tools. Entire cultures arose as a result of hunting one particular species of animal. An excellent example of this would be the North American Plains Indian culture. With the introduction of the horse to this continent, entire tribes took to the plains, and built a new culture surrounding the buffalo. History shows us that the intent to eliminate the vast bison herds of the West was a deliberate attempt to subdue and control the Native Americans of the Great Plains.

As North America was settled, primarily by Europeans and Africans, people found the bountiful wildlife of America fascinating. For hundreds of years, most people in Europe had been denied the privilege of hunting wild game because much of the forests belonged to the nobility, and if they dared to do so, they faced dire consequences. Africans, on the other hand, had long lived a hunting, fishing, and gathering lifestyle.

As the non-native people began to expand on the North American continent, the wild creatures they found provided for the majority of their needs. The fur trappers were the first to explore the New World, and the lessons they learned from the Native Americans kept them alive and relatively comfortable. They became known as "Mountain Men"—men clothed in brain-tanned buckskin (deer hides), ornamented in the Native style of additional animal parts and intricate beadwork. Although the Mountain Men were the first, they were not the last; market hunters and settlers came soon after, and by the 1840s the great fur trade of North America was waning as the result of over-harvest of the animals.

Lured by the Mountain Men's stories of the great number of wildlife still abundant in the woods and plains of North America, the market hunters followed. Market hunting was a profession that relied on the killing of vast numbers of wildlife to provide brief economic gain. There were many people who took to reaping the wild harvest that this new country could provide. These men and women shipped hundreds of thousands of animals and their parts "back East" to the lucrative markets awaiting them. Many species of wildlife were decimated, and some of those populations never recovered. The passenger pigeon was one of these animals. It was once the most populous creature to ever grace the face of the earth. In the mid-1800s there were an estimated 3 billion of these birds darkening the skies of this country. The last one, "Martha," died in the Cincinnati Zoo in 1914. No passenger pigeon has ever been seen since, but we now have city names such as Pigeon Roost, MS, as a reminder of what we have lost. More of these tales are told in an excellent book by Peter Matthiessen titled *Wildlife in America* (Viking Penguin Inc.).

By the late 1800s, Americans began to realize that the wildlife they had depended on and taken for granted, was disappearing. The alligators of the South were almost gone. In the 1890s it was declared that the wood duck would become extinct by the turn of the century. Deer were becoming rare in many states. The numerous bison of the Great Plains had been whittled down to a few dozen animals. The Carolina parakeet was almost gone, as was the heath hen of the coast of North Carolina. Zoology books in Europe listed sea turtles as "edible" or "non-edible" species. Once, while looking at a picture of a man sitting atop a huge pile of dead animals the man had slain, President Theodore Roosevelt remarked, "My, what a game hog!" Thus, an American colloquialism was born. People all across America looked and remembered what once was and realized that action was needed. Americans cried out to their state and Federal governments for a solution to the problem. The wildlife of America was disappearing at an alarming rate: without action, it would all too soon be gone forever!

As a result of the public outcry, laws were passed to protect threatened wildlife species. One of the first important wildlife laws enacted in this country was the Lacey Act of 1900, which prohibited the interstate transport of illegally taken wildlife. This law made it possible to stop those people who were unethically and illegally over-harvesting and transporting wildlife for monetary gain. Eventually other laws were passed, including the Migratory Bird Treaty Act of 1918, the Migratory Bird Hunting Stamp Act of 1934, and the Endangered Species Act of 1973. Each of these laws was designed to either protect specific species of animals from the threat of extinction, or to assure the continuance of healthy populations. Most of them have worked well. As a result of the Bald Eagle Protection Act of 1940, bald eagle populations have recovered to the point that they have been removed from the threatened and endangered status of the Endangered Species Act of 1973, though they still remain a protected species. This period of "America's Wildlife Awakening" has been vital for the continued existence of wildlife in the United States.

The turn of the century saw the world's women addicted to fashion, at any cost. The millinery industry provided feather-adorned hats for fashion conscious women, and this trade alone saw the creation of the world's first national wildlife refuge in

1903 with the establishment of the Pelican Island Refuge in Florida. President Theodore Roosevelt declared this small three-acre island a sanctuary to protect the pelicans and other wading birds that nested there from poachers who were killing the birds simply for their breeding feathers. Today, this National Wildlife Refuge still exists and will celebrate its 100th birthday as a refuge in March of 2003. The pelicans still nest there. The first manager of this refuge was a boat builder named Paul Kroegel, who lived adjacent to the small island off of the northeast Florida coast. Using his sailboat for transportation and armed with a 10-gauge shotgun, he enforced the "no hunting" laws of this new National Wildlife Refuge. Paul survived to retire, and did a fine job keeping the birds safe during his tenure.

Why are these 100-year-old laws important, and how have they helped America's wildlife? Well, today we look back at those laws passed and pay especial tribute to the men and women who gave their lives over the years trying to enforce those laws, and acknowledge that neither the laws nor the lives were not in vain! The wood duck is plentiful once again. The American alligator is no longer protected by the Endangered Species Act because its population has flourished. The American bison once again roams the Great Plains in vast herds (somewhat more constrained than years of old, but still roaming!). The eastern wild turkey is abundant, the waterfowl populations of the continent have rebounded, deer are now common throughout most of their historic ranges, and the list of success stories goes on.

Americans have always cherished the privileges we have as a society. For everything we lose as a people, we are willing to give up even more in order to regain what was lost, and once we regain that thing desired, we despise ever losing it again. The lessons of September 11, 2001 ("9-11") only reinforce this principle. On that tragic day in American history, we suffered terribly at the hands of foreign terrorism. We lost something precious: our sense of protection and immunity from the world's injustices. Yet immediately after that day of loss, we willingly gave up some of our precious fourth amendment constitutional rights (the freedom from unreasonable search and seizure) in order to someday feel safe and secure again.

As a nation, we deeply understand how our forefathers felt about losing the wildlife riches of this country we had so long enjoyed and desired to retain. As conscientious individuals, we must admit that without the laws of the last hundred years, many of the wildlife species we enjoy today would not be here. The laws of "old" have protected them so they endure today.

So how do these laws of old affect me, as a modern day Pagan interested only in possessing (not selling) these parts? You must know "up-front" that there are some animal parts that you will not be allowed to legally possess. This is not done to deprive you as a citizen, but rather to protect the species involved. Here's an example: Imagine you are driving down a remote rural Florida road. Imagine as well that there is a semi-truck in front of you, and you are both travelling the legal speed limit of 60 miles per hour. Suddenly, from the right, a mature bald eagle zooms after its prey, directly into the right front fender of the semi-truck. Horrible? Yes! You have a VERY strong totem affiliation for Eagle, and you are highly concerned about the bird, so you pull over. As you approach the bird, you realize the animal is already dead from a head injury. You pick it up, admire its regal beauty, stroke its luxuriant feathers, and breathe the aroma of its wildness. You feel sorrow? Yes! But now what? Can you have the bird, its feathers, its beak, or its claws?

Unfortunately no, for to do so would be a violation of Federal law. Bald eagles are protected under the Bald Eagle Protection Act of 1940. As a result of this and other laws and executive orders, all of the parts of this animal are illegal to possess for the average American. The reason for this is convoluted, but important. Long ago, before the Africans and Europeans, there were other indigenous people here in North America: the Native Americans. These people did, and still do, revere the eagle as a powerful totem animal whose mere presence is strong magick. The U.S. Government has recognized the significance of the eagle to native tribes, and now gives Native Americans preference to certain eagle parts. The Bald Eagle Repository in Denver, Colorado is the collecting facility for all eagle parts in North America. From this repository, eagle parts are divided and shared among all Native Americans, nationwide, that have a documented religious need for these parts.

So what is it that makes Native Americans' religious rights more important than mine? Well, the brutal answer is the court system. Native Americans fought for years to regain the right to practice their ancient religious beliefs, and they were able to prove in court through historical, ethnological, and anthropological records the basis for their needs. However, even with this right, and a Bureau of Indian Affairs (BIA) issued certificate of native birth, some Native American wait for years to receive eagle parts from the repository because only eagles that are accidentally killed or seized from poachers are available for distribution.

What could happen if you take that eagle home, pluck it, stuff it, mount it, and honor it? Well, if you are caught, you could face these current fines under Federal law:

Bald Eagle Protection Act of 1940, as amended 1978. Sec. 668. Bald and golden eagles.

"Whoever, within the United States or any place subject to the jurisdiction thereof, without being permitted to do so as provided in this subchapter, shall knowingly, or with wanton disregard for the consequences of his act take, possess, sell, purchase, barter, offer to sell, purchase or barter, transport, export or import, at any time or in any manner any bald eagle commonly known as the American eagle or any golden eagle, alive or dead, or any part, nest, or egg thereof of the foregoing eagles, or whoever violates any permit or regulation issued pursuant to this subchapter, shall be fined not more than $5,000 or imprisoned not more than one year or both: Provided, That in the case of a second or subsequent conviction for a violation of this section committed after October 23, 1972, such person shall be fined not more than $10,000 or imprisoned not more than two years...."

Fines and imprisonment of this type are necessary, in part, to keep "Joe Blow" from going out and shooting an eagle so he could sell the parts. If stopped by a law enforcement officer, "Joe Blow" could say he found those parts, and how would the officer prove otherwise? Eagle populations would suffer. The laws are designed to keep this from happening.

With all this in mind, what the heck do I do with the eagle? I can't keep it, but I don't want it to go to waste! First, remember that "waste" is a human-defined concept. Nothing goes to waste in the wild (just ask the dung beetle that needs those very real "wastes" found in the woods!). The best advice here is to leave the animal's carcass in a recognizable spot, then go call the local game and fish law enforcement folks. They will pick up the animal and make certain that the parts get to those who will not only revere it, but can also legally possess it.

What about the parts of nonFederally protected species, such as a box turtle shell? I want to make a rattle. Can I have that? Or I found a deer skull and want to keep that. Can I? Not to put you off, but it depends on the laws of the state where you live. The best advice would be to contact your local game and fish office to determine if a particular animal is legal to possess, because state law varies between states, and none of us want to get into trouble with the law. Animal parts you will never be allowed to possess are those specifically protected under Federal law, such as birds that migrate, which are covered by the Migratory Bird

Treaty Act mentioned previously herein. Also, any species listed in the Endangered Species Act are prohibited from possession.

Remember that the laws are not there just to cruelly deprive you from having an animal part. They are there to ensure that future generations of Americans and visitors to our nation can enjoy the many species that call this country "home." They are good laws, and they are laws that the ethical Pagan, and especially anyone interested in working with animal magick, should want to uphold.

Have these laws solved all of the problems? No, but they have solved some. Is there still a problem, and does more need to be done? Wildlife laws can be very confusing because it is a very diverse field. Most of these laws are there to protect our wildlife resources that are daily at risk. Last year, according to Interpol, it was estimated that the illegal trade in wildlife, and their parts, was second only to the illegal drug trade, and generated an estimated $6 billion dollars on the black market worldwide. The sad part about this bit of trivia is that the U.S. leads the world in this trade! In pet stores across America, South American parrots can sell for as much as $40,000 (some of these are captive bred, and legal for sale, but others are not). In the Shenandoah Valley of Virginia, a case by the Park Service in 1999, called Operation SOUP (Special Operation to Uncover Poaching), was made when officers seized 300 gallbladders taken from illegally harvested black bears. Once dried, shipped to the Orient, and sold by the gram, these gall bladders have a higher street value than cocaine. Many, if not all, of those bears were killed only for their gallbladders—the rest of the carcass was left to rot. Across America, and the world, threats to wildlife continue, and solid game laws are our primary tool in protecting these animals. A sad but true story comes from a 1994 *Time* magazine article. The article stated that in Hiroshima, Japan, the meat of humpback whales was seized in a supermarket, where it was expected to sell for several hundred dollars per plate. Yes! We need to do more!

How can you, as a member of the Pagan community, assist in doing away with this black market trade in wildlife? Here are a few suggestions: First, never buy articles made from illegally taken wildlife. If you are not sure, then ask the vendor, **and** ask for a receipt! That way, if an unscrupulous vendor duped you, and if you get into trouble with the law, you have proof that you thought it was legal. It then becomes the legal liability of the vendor. Second, know the laws in your local area. Become informed and educated, because apathy and ignorance has been the downfall of so many things in the past. Report violators, because they are stealing wildlife resources from you as well as everyone else. And finally, be personally responsible! If you are walking through the woods and find a hawk feather (protected by the Migratory Bird Treaty Act), leave it where it is. Look at it, respect it, wonder at it, but whatever you do, don't pick it up, put it in your hat, and parade around with it showing everyone what you found. Where is the respect for the animal or the laws that are trying to protect the animal in this type of behavior?

Remember the once plentiful salmon of the northwest U.S., the passenger pigeon of the East, the black bears of Louisiana, the sea cows of Alaska, and the bison of the Great Plains were driven to, or over, the brink of extinction by us. Let us never abuse our wildlife resources again!

Websites that can assist you in your search for understanding the legal avenues of the possession of wildlife parts are listed below. These sites can be of great value in clarifying the complex, sometimes confusing, but very valuable laws that protect one of America's greatest treasures—our wild natural resources!

Title 50 Code of Federal Regulations can be found at:
www.access.gpo.gov/nara/cfr/index.hrml

The homepage of the U.S. Fish and Wildlife Service can be found at: *www.fws.gov/*

The homepage for the U.S. Fish and Wildlife Service's Division of law enforcement can be found at: *www.le.fws.gov*

Websites for state game and fish agencies are best found by doing a search using the name of the state and keywords: game laws, game/wildlife, fish.

The website for the National Eagle Repository is: *http://www.le.fws.gov/Eagle_Repository.htm*

Application forms to obtain animal parts for use by Native Americans for religious purposes: *http://r6alph.irm.r6.fws.gov/www/fws/law/le65.html*

The website for other Native American wildlife part needs can be found at the National Wildlife Property Repository: *http://r6alph.irm.r6.fws.gov/www/fws/law/le64.html*

Applicants to possess eagle parts must possess a certificate from the Bureau of Indian Affairs that they are Indian. Legal requirements for this can be found at: *http://www.doi.gov/bia/information/eaglepermi*

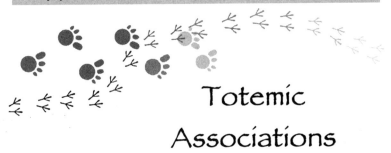

Totemic Associations

For those of you looking for a little more information to round out your understanding of animal symbolism, this appendix should prove helpful. Keep in mind as you read that this is but a brief overview of the global lore, history, and science of these creatures. We strongly encourage doing more research on your own regarding any animal or animal spirit that you hold close to your heart.

Ant

> phylum Arthropoda: class Insecta: order Hymenoptera: family Formicidae: 3,500 species

Chinese stories reveal the ant as a symbol of order, virtue, and service. They were worshipped in Thessaly, and Myrmidons claimed the ant as an ancestor spirit. In North American Shamanism the ant often represents patience and the ability to build (literally from the ground up), whereas in Central America various colors of ants indicate tribal affiliations. Finally, in China, Persia, India, and Greece huge ants act as guardians of important treasures, which may account for the fact that some people regard them as lucky.

Ass/Donkey

> phylum Chordata: class Mammalia: order
> Perissodactyla: family Equidae: three species

Egyptians and Assyrians both considered the donkey a humble creature. In Egypt, specifically, this creature was sacred to Set, and the wild ass of desert regions typified hermitage, caution, and solitude. Greeks felt that Dionysos protected the Ass. Being a beast of burden, many sacred processionals included these animals, and depictions of divine beings often showed an Ass as a means of transportation. For example, the Roman Vestalia includes decorated donkeys, and the portraits of the Chinese Immortal Chang Kwo-lao shows him riding a magickal donkey. Interestingly enough, in the East we see this creature as strong, brave, and intelligent, while in Western society it typifies stupidity and stubbornness.

Badger

> phylum Chordata: class Mammalia: order
> Carnivora: superfamily Canoidea: family
> Mustelidae: subfamily Taxidiinae, Mellivorinae,
> Melinae: six species in five genera

Myths claim that a badger's age is indicated by the number of holes in its tail (one hole per year). In China this creature is aligned with the moon and typifies playfulness and magickal power. Similarly, in Japan, the Badger is a trickster who is a powerful illusionist. Moving westward we find the Hopi placing the badger in the North of the sacred circle, and several clans are named after this animal. Finally, among the Zuni the badger is the keeper of medicine roots and guardian of the southern region of the medicine wheel.

Bat

> phylum Chordata: class Mammalia: order
> Chiroptera: families Phyllostomideae,
> Vespertillionidae, Molossidae: 925 species

As a creature of the darkness it's not surprising to discover that the bat has very conflicting symbolism. Egyptians used bat head charms to prevent pigeons from leaving their coves. In China bats are an emblem of Show-Hsing, the god of longevity, and they represent luck, health, wealth, peace, and happiness. American Indian lore holds the bat as a symbol of rebirth or initiation, while in New Zealand it's a harbinger of bad luck and Western stories associate this creature with vampires and death.

Bear

> phylum Chordata: class Mammalia: order
> Carnivora: family Ursidae: nine species in six
> genera

Archaeological studies indicate that even Neanderthal man had shrines to the Bear. In a variety of shamanic settings as widespread as Japan and Siberia, Bear was the Master of animals who also taught the Shamans. American Indians place Bear in the western quarter of the Circle, having a strong will and heart. Here they bear messages from the forest to people, and symbolize supernatural powers. Names for the Bear spirit reflect the global reverence. Two examples are King of the Forest (Ainus) and Grandfather (Lapps). Among the Scandinavian and Teutonic peoples the bear is sacred to Thor, while the Celts associate it with the Goddess.

Beaver

> phylum Chordata: class Mammalia: order
> Rodentia: family Castoridae: two species in one
> genera (*Castor canadensis*: beaver and *Castor
> fiber*: European beaver)

Native American stories place the beaver in the Council of Animals alongside Otter, Hare, and Spider as helpmates for humankind and light-bringers. Among both the Seneca and

Iroquois tribes beaver symbolizes home, family, or the accomplishments of a group. European symbolism similarly depicts Beaver as industrious, vigilant, and peace loving.

Bee

> phylum Arthropoda: class Insecta: order
> Hymenoptera: superfamily Apoidea:
> 3,500+ species

In Chapter 3 we briefly discussed Bees as messengers to the gods alongside several other winged creatures. Perhaps this is how the phrase "the telling of bees" began. In Greece the bee was sacred to Cupid, because they ravish flowers and kiss the hearts of the plants, which might explain why a bee sting had phallic connections and why mead (honey wine) became a lover's beverage. This symbolic value isn't unique. It reappears in the Indian god of love, Kama, where the bee representing sweet pain. Returning our attention to Greece, however, we discover that bees were called the Birds of the Muses, and thus we come by the connection between bees, honey, and creative power. Bees bless poets and artists alike, and eloquent speakers have "honey on their lips." In the Qu'ran they're depicted as dependable, intelligent, and wise.

Boar

> phylum Chordata: class Mammalia: order
> Artiodactyla: suborder Suina: families Suidae and
> Tayassuidae: 16 species in eight genera

In Vedic writings, the storm god Ruda held the title of "the boar of the sky." With similar ferocity, Greco-Roman myths associate this creature with Ares and Mars. In Celtic art anywhere the Boar and Bear are depicted together it represents both the conflicts between, and balance of, spiritual and temporal power (the boar being spiritual, and a symbol of not only magick, but also an individual's life force). Among Persians, the shining boar is the sun, and this creature was supposedly created to protect humans from serpents. Lastly, in Japan, the boar is a lunar animal associated with the best warrior qualities.

Buffalo

> phylum Chordata: class Mammalia: order Artiodactyla: family Bovidae: subfamily Bovinae: four species in three genera

In the sacred texts of the Vedas, buffalo are associated with Vana, the god of the dead, who rises a buffalo. This connection between life and death also comes up among the Zulu people who say a person's soul can pass into a buffalo. However, by far the greatest prevalence of Buffalo symbolism comes from Native American traditions where it represents supernatural power, strength, diligence, and appears as the totem of several tribes. In some stories it was Buffalo who taught people how to pray.

Bull/Cow

> phylum Chordata: class Mammalia: order Artiodactyla: suborder Ruminantia: family Bovidae
>
> *Bos taurus* (domestic cow)

A prevalent symbol in pastoral and agricultural societies, Bull was among the first worshipped creatures being honored for its strength, fertility, and usefulness. Bull cults appear in Sumer-Semetic regions, all of which revered the Bull's virility. Zoroastrian (Persia) says the bull was the first created creature, and they, too, held it as a symbol of generative energy, as did the Hindus, Celts, and Greeks, who often had wild bulls at pre-Olympic rituals for its potency and physical power. Perhaps the greatest region of Bull veneration, however, was Egypt, where the Pharaohs themselves were called Bulls, and where the bull-headed god Apis (god of fertility) was worshipped.

Butterfly

> phylum Arthropoda: subphylum Uniramia: class
> Insecta: order Lepidoptera: 125,000+ known
> species in order

It is almost universally accepted that the butterfly represents rebirth and renewal. In China and Japan a butterfly further symbolizes longevity, joy, and leisure, especially when combined with a chrysanthemum. Moving further west we find Greco-Roman tradition associating this beautiful insect with the Horae, the spirit of the seasons, and with the soul, which was often represented as a butterfly in Greek renderings.

Camel

> phylum Chordata: class Mammalia: order
> Artiodactyla: suborder Tylopoda: families Camels
> and Llamas: two species of camels and four
> species of llamas

African peoples regard the camel as an emblem of service and obedience, as well as a water guide and guardian. Being a very valuable animal in the Middle East, Arabian myths illustrate camels as a creature of providence and nobility. Islam even places it as an animal of Paradise.

Cat

> phylum Chordata: class Mammalia: order
> Carnivora: superfamily Feloidae: family Felidae:
> subfamilies Acinonychinae (one species), Felinae
> (28 species in 12 genera), and Pantherinae (eight
> species in three genera)

> *Felis silvestris* (domestic cat)

The changing dilation of a cat's eyes made this creature into both a solar and lunar animal. It bears the strength of the sun and the transforming nature of the moon. Black cats, in particular, are associated with Witches, who gain their power from the moon. These cats are said to be psychic and bonded to their human companion. The intensity of worship was such that thousands of cats have been found mummified with their owners as protectors and guides in the afterlife. In Scandinavia cats are an attribute of Freyja, in North America wild cats are associated with the hunter god, in Hindu tradition Shasti (the goddess of birth) rides a cat, and the Peruvian cat Ccoa is a storm spirit.

Chameleon

> phylum Chordata: class Reptilia: order Squamata: suborder Sauria (Lacertilia): infraorder Iguanidae: family Chamaeleonidae

Chameleon is often associated with the Element of Air because of its changing colors (seemingly at whim). In African tradition Chameleon gave humans the message of immortality, and in West Africa the creature is thought to have magickal qualities, specifically in weather magick, where it has the ability to bring rain.

Cock

> phylum Chordata: class Aves: subclass Neornithes: order Galliformes: family Phasianidae: 214 species in 15 genera in three subfamilies (includes pheasants, partridges, francolins, quail, turkeys, grouse, and guinea fowl)

> *Gallus domesticus* (common domestic chicken)

Because it crows at the dawn the Cock has strong solar attributes, including courage and alertness. White cocks were sacred to Athene, Demeter, and Apollo. Yellow cocks were offered to Anubis and Osiris in Egypt. Scandinavian lore places a golden cock at the top of the Tree of Life to guard against evil, while Romans observed these creatures in various forms of divination (especially before important battles). Chinese see the cock as a lucky bird that wards off malevolent spirits, and as the embodiment of yang energy because it typifies bravery, valor, and devotion, especially in aggressive settings. Meanwhile, in Japan, Shinto tradition uses the symbol of a cock on a drum to call people to prayer.

Coyote

> phylum Chordata: class Mammalia: order
> Carnivora: family Canidae: one species
>
> *Canis lat*rans (coyote)

The classical trickster in North Amerindian tradition, but most strongly in the Plains region. Being the thief of fire and spirit of the night, Coyote also has magickal powers blended with a great love for humor and poetry. Among the Hopi, Coyote is credited for creating the Milky Way when he let stars escape from a sealed pot, which is an excellent illustration of this creature's odd dichotomy (negligence/creation, teacher/ trickster, etc.).

Crab

> phylum Arthropoda: subphylum Crustacea: class
> Malacostraca: order Decapoda: 10,000+ species
> in the order

Most obvious is the crab's association with the sun sign Cancer. It's interesting to note that the sun moves retrograde through this constellation after the Summer Solstice, which may be why Buddhism associates the crab with the cycle of death and rebirth. In Sumeria, crabs are sacred to Nina, the Lady of the Waters, and in Inca society with the Great Mother (specifically during the waning moon). Among some Melanesian clans, the crab is a totem that may not be eaten out of respect.

Crane

> phylum Chordata: class Aves: order Gruiformes:
> family Gruidae: 15 species in two genera

Typically, Crane is another messenger spirit who is often credited with being smart, disciplined, and watchful. The Chinese often use cranes in symbolism as an intermediary between the worlds. As the carrier of souls it represents luck, happiness, and honor. Japanese people seem similarly enamored of this bird calling it "Honorable Lord Crane." In Ainu mythology, Crane bore clothing and other necessities to humans from heaven. Native Americans connect it with wisdom and longevity, and in European heraldry it symbolized either vigilance or strong family lineage.

Cricket/Grasshopper

> phylum Arthropoda: subphylum Uniramia: class
> Insecta: order Orthoptera: 23,000+ species in the
> order

These spirits are most venerated in Eastern cultures. In Japan, for example, the song of the cricket is likened to the chant of the Buddhist priests. Among the Chinese it represents the season of Summer and bravery. Both Chinese and Japanese homes keep crickets as pets for luck in the home.

Crocodile/Alligator

> phylum Chordata: class Reptilia: Subclass
> Archosauria: order Crocodylia: suborder
> Eusuchia: families Crocodylidae and
> Alligatoridae: 21 species

Crocodiles seem to have ambivalent symbolism. In Egypt, for example, they represented sunrise and thus the Pharaohs as well as Typhon (the power of evil). Crocodiles were also sacred to both Ra (the sun god) and Set (a brutal god). African

Bantus used crocodiles in magick; in Sumatra the creature is worshipped as a dangerous God; and in Mayan festivals, crocodiles became an effigy.

Crow/Raven

> phylum Chordata: class Aves: order Passeriformes: family Corvidae: 107 species (includes jays, crows, ravens, magpies, nutcrackers, and jackdaws)
>
> *Corvus corax* (common raven)

Crows and ravens have a great deal of overlapping symbolism in part because they look a lot alike and are often mistaken for each other. Egyptian mythology uses two crows to symbolize a happy marriage; in Greece, crows are sacred to Apollo; and Japanese Shinto tradition associates them with the temples as messengers of the gods. White crows appear in Celtic lore as Branwen (sister of Bran), medieval bestiaries consider crow a soothsayer, and American Indians often mention the crow as the keeper of Law and creation's Mysteries.

Looking to the Raven by comparison, it is similar to the crow because it has prophetic value (Ravens were said to foretell Plato's death), and even protected people with the gift of site in Old Testament writings. Zorastrianism and Mithraism both revere the bird as a servant of the sun; in Greek tradition it's the Sun God's messenger; and in Viking custom it bore missives from Odin. Finally, in Native American lore, he is a trickster, shape-shifter, and culture hero who created both day and night.

Deer

> phylum Chordata: class Mammalia: order Artiodactyla: suborder Ruminantia: family Cervidae: 44 species in 17 genera

Egyptian temples to Isis depicted deer as sacred animals until the creature died out in that region. Among Christians, the Hart, or Hind, portrays love and agility. Greeks believed the deer to be sacred to Artemis, while the Vedas attribute it to the God of the Wind. In China deer represent noble rank, success, and prosperity; among the Celts deer are vehicles that transport souls to the otherworld; and several Native American tribes have Deer totems or clans.

Dog

phylum Chordata: class Mammalia: order Carnivora: family Canidae: 34 species in 14 genera (Canines, general)

Canis lupus familiaris (domestic dog)

Dogs were domesticated around 7500 B.C.E. As the first animal companion, it's not surprising that they became associated with loyalty, friendship, and protection. In Phoenician art dogs are associated with Astarte; in Egypt, with Anubis; and in Greece, with Aesculapius (the great healer). The sacred writings of Zorastrianism (the Avesta) indicate the dog is wise, vigilant, and devoted. Celtic myth includes dogs as companions to Epona the horse goddess and Nodens, the god of healing; while in Scandinavia they are the counselors and messengers of Odin.

Dolphin

phylum Chordata: class Mammalia: order Cetacea: suborder Odontoceti (toothed whales): families Delphinidae (ocean dolphins: 22 species in 10 genera), Phocoenidae (porpoises: six species in four genera), and Platanistidae (river dolphins: five species in four genera)

Tursiops truncatus (bottlenose dolphin)

Dolphins represent the power of the sea and swiftness. The sun god Apollo is always shown with dolphins in his temple, and he could take their form. Sumero-Semitic people consider the dolphin a representation of Ea-Oannes, while Romans depict Cupid with these creatures. In Christianity, a dolphin accompanying a ship symbolizes Christ guiding the church. Amazon tribes feel dolphins can change into humans at will and go dancing, while Native Americans see it as the embodiment of the Great Spirit and vital breath.

Dragonfly

phylum Arthropoda: subphylum Uniramia: class Insecta: order Odonata: 5,000 species (dragonflies and damselflies)

This is the national emblem of Japan and appears regularly in Japanese art as a symbol of immortality. In the West, American Indians typify this creature as swift, busy, and an illusionist.

Duck

phylum Chordata: class Aves: order Anseriformes: family Anatidae: 158 species in 46 genera (includes ducks, geese, and swans)

Pliny called ducks "wind prophets." In Egypt it was sacred to Isis; and in Greece, to Poseidon. In China it's an emblem of marital happiness, fidelity, and loveliness, and Native Americans see it as a mediator between Sky and Water.

Eagle

phylum Chordata: class Aves: order Falconiformes: family Accipitridae): 220 species in 59 genera (includes hawks, eagles, and Old World vultures)

Haliaeetus leucocephalus (Bald eagle)

Eagles have strong ties with many sky gods as a symbol of the sun, power, authority, leadership, honor, and success. Included in this list we find Ninurta (Babylonian sun god), Marduk (Assyrian sun god), Odin (Norse), Nasi (Arabic supreme god), and Zeus/Jupiter (Greece/Rome). Spiritually speaking this animal reminds us of the human desire to soar upward in our Path. Hebrews regard Eagle as the symbol of the East and new beginnings or renewal; while in Japan, the Golden Eagle is a type of the Great Spirit who never touches the earth because of his great beauty, and who guards the Ainu people.

Eel

> phylum Chordata: subphylum Vertebrata:
> superclass Gnathostomata: class Osteichthyes:
> subclass Actinopterygii: superorder Teleostei:
> order Anguilliformes: 597 species in the order

Ancient Greeks venerated eels, and Phoenicians had temples to their war god decorated with eel imagery. Typically in oceanic settings this creature has strong erotic overtones, being a phallic symbol of carnal love.

Elephant

> phylum Chordata: class Mammalia: order
> Proboscidea: family Elephantidae: two species

> *Elephas maximus* (Asian) and *Loxodonta africana* (African)

Common interpretive values for the elephant include cognitive abilities (specifically memory), long-suffering, wisdom, and devotion. Greek art shows Dionysos riding an elephant-drawn chariot, which symbolized immortality. In Rome, the elephant appeared on coins to illustrate imperial power. Hinduism has the wise god Ganesha who bears an elephant's head, and elephants were sacred to the Buddha. In China, white elephants represent strength, endurance, prudence, and sovereignty.

Elk/Stag

> phylum Chordata: class Mammalia: order
> Artiodactyla: family Cervidae: one species of
> "elk"—*Cervus elaphus* (elk, wapiti, red deer); and
> two species commonly associated with "stag"—
> *Dama dama* (Fallow deer) and the extinct
> *Megaloceros* (Irish elk)

Siberians and Native Americans alike associate the elk with strength, the warrior spirit, and mystical power. The stag appears in the Tree of Life as a symbol of good overcoming evil. In Greece, the stag was sacred to Artemis and Dionysos, while the Celts associated it with Cernunnos, and thus, fertile energies.

Fox

> phylum Chordata: class Mammalia: order
> Carnivora: family Canidae: 16 species in six
> genera

Fox is another trickster figure in the animal kingdom, being filled with cunning and having the ability to shapeshift. The first time we see the fox appearing as a trickster is in Sumeria, where a fox rescues the god Enki. Bacchus is associated with the fox, too, probably because of this god's rather roguish nature. Bestiaries give the fox credit for his craftiness and begin using the phrase "get foxed" as an allusion to being fooled effectively. Chinese and Japanese stories alike indicate the fox can become human at will, and sometimes can be enticed to help humans if the creature finds the task at least somewhat amusing.

Frog

> phylum Chordata: class Amphibia: order Anura:
> family Ranidae (true frogs): 3400 species in
> 301 genera in 21 families (toads and frogs)

Known to be a bringer of rain, the Egyptians associate frogs with Hekt (the goddess of water), along with Isis and Hathor (the Mother and fertile goddess). The Chinese have a frog spirit named Ch'ing-Wa Sheng that they worship as a healer, or propitiate to encourage professional success and wealth. Greeks used frogs as a symbol of harmonious relationships and fertility, and an emblem of Aphrodite. Celts connect the frog with healing, as did many Shamanic peoples. Placing a frog in someone's mouth when they had a cold and having it hop away was a common cure (thus the phrase "a frog in my throat").

Goat

> phylum Chordata: class Mammalia: order Artiodactyla: suborder Ruminantia: family Bovidae:
>
> > subfamily Caprinae: one species—*Oreamnos americanus* (mountain goat)
> >
> > subfamily Hippotraginae: two species of antelope
> >
> > subfamily Antilopinae: 17 species of antelope in 10 genera
> >
> > > one species "true goat"—*Capra aegagrus*

Male goats are the ultimate symbol of male virility. Interchangeable with Gazelles and Antelopes symbolically, goats also represent health and creativity. Goats were sacred to Artemis, Zeus, Pan, and Dionysos in Greece. Arabic myths associate this creature with personal dignity and honor.

Goose

> phylum Chordata: class Aves: order Anseriformes: family Anatidae: 158 species in 46 genera (includes ducks, geese, and swans)

Unlike the saying "silly goose," geese were a well-respected creature in ancient times and they were sacred to many deities including Hera (Greece), Apollo (Greece), Mars (Rome), Juno (Rome), Amon-Ra (Egypt), and Epona (Gaelic tradition). According to Egyptian myths it was a goose that laid the cosmic egg from which all things came. In China and Japan it's a messenger spirit, bearing good news.

Hawk

> phylum Chordata: class Aves: order Falconiformes: family Accipitridae: 220 species in 59 genera (includes hawks, eagles, and Old World vultures)

Hawk is a great solar bird able to fly to the sun without fear. Not surprisingly, this bird was sacred to Ra in Egypt, Apollo in Greece (and also worked as his messenger), and to Ormuzd in Persia, all of whom are solar figures. Native American lore tells us that after the flood Hawk helped create the world.

Hippopotamus

> phylum Chordata: class Mammalia: order Artiodactyla: suborder Suina: family Hippopotamidae: two species in two genera

A somewhat popular figure in Egyptian mythology, the hippo is associated with Amenti the Great Mother as well as the goddess Rera, who is portrayed as an upright hippo. The Behemoth of the Old Testament is thought to be a hippo. Generally speaking, this creature is associated with Water energy and fertility, especially if depicted pregnant.

Horse

> phylum Chordata: class Mammalia: order Perissodactyla: family Equidae: nine species in one genus (includes horses, asses, and zebras)

As discussed earlier, Horse has both solar and lunar associations. The white horse of the sea typifies the watery gods and powers, while horses of gold or fire embrace the solar gods. In Hindu stories the last incarnation of Vishnu, called Kalki, appeared as a white horse that brought peace. It's not uncommon to see horses pulling the vehicles for various Deities, too, including Mithra (Iranian god of light), Apollo (Greco-Roman Sun god), Anahita (Semitic goddess of victory), and Surya (Vedic sun god). In winged form horses represent honor, eloquence, creativity, and the soaring imagination. Muslims see the horse as a god-sent animal, and in Christian art they represent the movement of the soul from darkness to light and courage.

Hummingbird

> phylum Chordata: class Aves: order
> Apodiformes: family Trochilidae: 319 species in
> 109 genera

Frequently associated with harmony, joy, and grace, hummingbirds are said to have magickal qualities, and this creature's feathers were a common component in love spells. Mayan stories tell us that this bird knows the answer to the riddle of duality, while the Native Americans watch this bird carefully to learn the dance that would once again give animals dominion over the earth (instead of the white man).

Jaguar

> phylum Chordata: class Mammalia: order
> Carnivora: superfamily Feloidea: family Felidae:
> subfamily Pantherinae: one species
>
> *Panthera onca* (jaguar)

As the third largest feline in the world, the magickal power of this creature has long been venerated. In Central and Southern American mythology jaguar symbolism is prevalent.

Offerings were made regularly to a Jaguar god who could turn into human form. Shamans could be possessed by Jaguar, and after death he could become one himself.

Lamb/Sheep

> phylum Chordata: class Mammalia: order Artiodactyla: suborder Ruminantia: family Bovidae: subfamily Caprinae: six species in four genera

One of the most popular items for offerings, lambs symbolize the spiritual novice, innocence, and purity. By comparison, sheep seem to imply the need to be lead and a timid nature. The Egyptian goddess Ament bore a sheep's head. Greeks and Romans associated sheep with numerous gods and goddesses and used them as sacrifices. Among Muslims it's a holy animal; and in China, Huang Ch'u-Ping was the god of sheep typically worshipped by shepherds.

Leopard

> phylum Chordata: class Mammalia: order Carnivora: superfamily Feloidea: family Felidae: subfamily Pantherinae: three species in three genera

> *Panthera pardus* (leopard): *Neofelis nebulosa* (clouded leopard): *Panthera uncia* (snow leopard)

In the Old Testament this feline symbolized vitality, quickness, cunning, and fortitude. Egyptians associated it with Osiris and the priests of this god are often illustrated as wearing leopard skins. In China, Leopard represents courage and the warrior spirit; and in Africa, the leopard is a cult animal sacred to several tribes and is given the attribute of fertility.

Lion

> phylum Chordata: class Mammalia: order Carnivora: superfamily Feloidea: family Felidae: subfamily Pantherinae: one species

Panthera leo (lion)

Lions are solar (Leo is a sun sign), and filled with leadership, power, vitality, strength, and honor. As an interesting balance to this masculine overtone, lions are featured as work-creatures for various goddesses in regions as far removed as Sumeria, Tibet, Crete, and Lycia, all of whom show the Great Mother with a chariot drawn by lions. In Egypt, a golden lion is an aspect of Ra, while a lion with a crescent is Osiris. In Babylon, Ishtar stands on lions and Hinduism tells us that a lion was the fourth avatar of Vishnu. Lions defend Buddhist law; and in Rome lion imagery was common at tombs to represent the power of life over death.

Lizard

> phylum Chordata: class Reptilia: order
> Squamata: suborder Lacertilia: family Iguanidae

Greeks and Egyptians alike identified the lizard with sagacity and luck. In Amazon regions, lizards are highly regarded as one aspect of the Master of Animals. In this region, lizard tails are considered to bear potent magick. Polynesian myths associate green lizards with Moko who protects fishing, and specifically in Hawaii the lizard is honored as an ancestral spirit. Finally, in some Native American traditions this creature is a dream-teacher.

Monkey

> phylum Chordata: class Mammalia: order
> Primates: 233 species in 13 families (including
> humans: *Homo sapiens*) in order

The monkey god Vayu of Hinduism has the power of courage, quickness, service, and strength. Buddhists say it was an early incarnation of the Buddha, and it's from Japanese myth that we get the Mizaru (the monkeys who portray "see no evil," "hear no evil," and "speak no evil"). Mayan tradition shows the god of the North Star with a monkey's head, and in West Africa some monkeys are not to be touched in the belief that they embody human souls.

Mouse

> phylum Chordata: class Mammalia: order
> Rodentia (2,000 species in 30 families): suborder
> Sciurognathi (11 families): family Muridae
> (1,325 species in 281 genera): subfamily Murinae
> (15 species in 11 genera)
>
> *Mus musculus* (house mouse)

Greek tradition associates Mouse with Zeus and Apollo. Aesop depicted mice as being both strong and weak, depending on necessity. Typical symbolisms for this creature include prudence, order, and intense observation.

Octopus

> phylum Mollusca: class Cephalopoda (octopus
> and squid): 650 species in the class

The spiral of this creature gave it associations with the moon and the eight-pointed Wheel of the Year. In Polynesian myth the octopus was responsible for both fire and water. In Samoa it's a sacred creature.

Otter

> phylum Chordata: class Mammalia: order
> Carnivora: superfamily Canoidea: family
> Mustelidae: subfamily Lutrinae: 11 species in
> seven genera

Otter is a sacred creature to Ormuzd (Zoroastrainism), and a cult animal in Peru. Native Americans connect Otter with the spirit of play, the Element of Water, and feminine powers. Among the Celts, Cernunnos has an otter companion.

Owl

> phylum Chordata: class Aves: order
> Strigiformes: families Strigidae ("true owls"—
> 178 species) and Tytonidae (17 species in two
> genera)

Athena often has an owl companion in Greek art. It was also sacred to Demeter and a magickal bird among the Celts. In the Vedas, Owl is a messenger spirit. This is also true in some Native American traditions, such as those of the Hopi, where finding an owl feather acts as a gentle reminder to be true to self.

Parrot

> phylum Chordata: class Aves: order
> Psittaciformes: family Psittacidae: 357 species in
> 79 genera

Among Brahmins, this bird is sacred because of its vocal power, while in Hindu tradition it's an attribute of the love god Kama, and also regarded as a rain prophet. Rome had a parrot cult, and among Hopis there is a Parrot clan that is second only to the Bear clan in importance.

Peacock

> phylum Chordata: class Aves: order Galliformes:
> family Phasianidae: two species
>
> *Pavo cristatus* (common peacock)

One of the loveliest descriptions of this bird comes from Ovid, who describes it as having the stars in its tail and the vault of heavens in its eyes. Among Romans it was the symbol of Juno, in Egyptian art it stands by Isis, and the goddess of wisdom, Sarasvati, rides a peacock in the Vedic writings. In Babylon and Persia they symbolize royalty and leadership, and in China and Japan—beauty and favor.

196 🐂 Animal Spirit

Rabbit/Hare

> phylum Chordata: class Mammalia: order
> Lagomorpha: family Leporidae: 54 species in
> 11 genera

Typically associated with the moon and fertility, in many cultures the "man" in the moon is often replaced with a hare. Among Romans, Aphrodite, Eros, and Cupid all were connected with this creature, and sometimes Hermes as well (in this case as a messenger spirit). Teutonic art shows the goddess Eostra (from whom we get the name Easter), holding a hare, and thus we come by our Easter "bunny." Hares, in China, represent the ultimate feminine power; Buddhism associates them with self-sacrifice; among Native Americans there is Manabozho, a Hare who is also a Creator; and in West Africa, Rabbit is a trickster type. The wearing of animal skins denotes humility and gentleness.

Ram

> phylum Chordata: class Mammalia: order
> Artiodactyla: suborder Ruminantia: family
> Bovidae: subfamily Caprinae: six species in
> four genera

Where the rabbit was lunar, the ram is definitively solar, carrying the symbolic value of virility and masculine power. Due to the spiraling horns of this creature it's often associated with thunder gods and the zodiacal sign of Capricorn. In Egypt Ra was addressed as a ram, among the Greeks it was a suitable offering to Zeus and sacred to Dionysos, and Agni, the Vedic god of fire, has a ram that symbolizes the sacred flames of Hindu tradition.

Salmon

> phylum Chordata: subphylum Vertebrata:
> superclass Gnathostomata: class Osteichthyes:
> subclass Actinopterygii: superorder Teleostei:
> order Salmoniformes: 320 species in the order

Believed by scientists to be one of the oldest creatures on this planet, the salmon seems particularly important to Celtic people, who connected it with sacred wells, sagacity, and prophesy. Eating this fish insures knowledge and keen senses. In North American Native tradition, salmon represents the cycle of death and rebirth, and it's often called upon as a guardian power.

Seal

> phylum Chordata: class Mammalia: order
> Carnivora/Pinnipedia: family Otariidae:
> 14 species in seven genera

Romans used sealskins as an anti-thunderstorm charm, potentially based on the writings of Pliny who said the seal was never struck by lightning. European myth connects the seal with ancestral spirits.

Serpent/Snake

> phylum Chordata: class Reptilia: order
> Squamata: suborder Ophidia/Serpentes:
> superfamilies Typhlopoidea, Henophidia,
> and Xenophidia: 2,000+ species

Because of its venom and dwelling on or under the ground, serpents and snakes have a very mixed reputation. It can be lunar, solar, male, female, positive, or negative, depending on the culture and era examined. Ishtar has a serpent companion, in Canaan it symbolized healing (which is how we come by the later emblem of healers the Caduceus), and in Egypt the cobra represented Ra as the ultimate Divinity. Greeks and Romans both kept snakes as pets for health and fertility knowing it was a sacred creature to great gods and goddesses such as Zeus, Apollo, Hermes, and Athene. Celtic people connect serpents with Cernunnos for virility, while Hindu tradition gives it the symbolic value of cosmic power, specifically transformation and creation. Polynesians have the Rainbow Serpent, a celestial creator Spirit, and Aztecs have Quetzalcoatl (the god of wisdom) who appears as a feathered serpent.

Shark

> phylum Chordata: subphylum Vertebrata:
> superclass Gnathostomata: class Chondrichthyes:
> subclass Elasmobranchii: order Euselachii (true
> sharks)

Polynesians believe that sharks may carry the souls of departed leaders and heroes. Hawaiians had shark gods who received worship, and were thought to have great mystical and magickal powers. It was also sacred to several West African tribes.

Snail

> phylum Mollusca: class Gastropoda:
> 90,000 species in the class

Because snails retreat into and emerge from their shells, they became a symbol of rebirth. Some people also consider them lucky, and observe their movements in divination. In Mayan tradition it's sacred to the moon god (Tecciztecatl), and also often appears in Aztec art as a head upon various gods.

Spider

> phylum Arthropoda: subphylum Chelicerata:
> class Arachnida: order Araneae: 35,000 species in
> the order

As the weaver of fate's web, Spider has some potent symbolism for such a tiny creature. Nearly every lunar goddess has a Spider attribute, as do many deities associated with destiny. Among them we find the Egyptian Neith, the Babylonian Ishtar, the Greek Athene, and the Norse Norns. Hinduism and Buddhism both characterize Spider as an illusionist and creator. In Africa the spider god is wise and great, but it can also be a trickster spirit. In Native American stories Spider Woman created the first alphabet, giving it associations with both communication and networking. Overall, spiders are thought lucky, especially for finances.

Squirrel

> phylum Chordata: class Mammalia: order Rodentia: family Sciuridae: subfamily Petauristinae (flying squirrels—six species in five genera): subfamily Sciurinae (tree and ground squirrels—34 species in nine genera)

Scandinavians position Squirrel in the Tree of Life as a mischief-maker. In Ireland the symbolism is more positive, being sacred to the goddess Medb (who personifies sovereignty). The Norse see Squirrel as a bringer of rain, while Amazonian tribes connect it with Fire and the master of the animals, Desaria. It is among the list of potential Witch animals from the Middle Ages.

Stork

> phylum Chordata: class Aves: order Ciconiiformes: family Ciconiidae: 19 species in six genera

Egyptian stories honor this bird as a protector of the elderly, and thus give it the symbolic value of loyalty and a keeper of laws. Greek myths have a stork goddess who brings and nourishes life, and it's sacred to Hera in this region. In Rome it's the bird of Juno.

Swallow

> phylum Chordata: class Aves: order Passeriformes: family Hirundinidae: eight species in seven genera

Babylonian myths replace the Dove of Noah's ark with a swallow. Chinese consider swallows as symbolic of bravery, loyalty, success, devotion, and joy. Bestiaries talk of the bird's attention to detail, and as a harbinger of Spring, many Europeans associated it with hope.

Swan

> phylum Chordata: class Aves: order
> Anseriformes: family Anatidae: 158 species in
> 46 genera (includes ducks, geese, and swans):
> three species of *Cygnus* genus

The swan·is connected with the Muse, specifically singing, thanks to the idea that upon its death the swan sings an incredibly beautiful song. Thus it was that Shakespeare received the title "swan of Avon." In Greece it's sacred to Aphrodite. Hindus carved them on temple walls to illustrate spirit, as Brahma rides a swan or goose, either one of which birthed the cosmic egg. Celts honored the swan as a solar bird with magickal and musical abilities, while Native Americans characterize them as trusting and graceful.

Swine/Boar

> phylum Chordata: class Mammalia: order
> Artiodactyla: suborder Suina: families Suidae and
> Tayassuidae: 16 species in eight genera

One of the most common lunar animals found globally, swine usually bore the symbolic value of prosperity and fertility. It was sacred to Isis in Egypt, Mars in Rome, and Keridwen among the Celts, who herself was a sow goddess. Keridwen was so important in some regions of Scotland that people abstained from eating the flesh of swine. Tibetan Buddhists associate Swine with the Mother Goddess, and in Oceanic regions it's often considered a shapeshifter.

Tiger

> phylum Chordata: class Mammalia: order
> Carnivora: superfamily Feloidea: family Felidae:
> subfamily Pantherinae: two species

> *Panthera tigris* (tiger) and *Panthera tigris altaica*
> (Siberian)

Eastern custom places Tiger as the King of Beasts instead of Lion. Here it symbolizes leadership, courage, ferocity, and power. In India it's common to sit on tiger skin during meditation; while in China, Tiger embodies the ultimate male energies including prowess and authority. It also has connections with the God of Wealth, the Goddess of Wind, and the constellation Orion. Japanese stories associate Tiger with the warrior spirit.

Turtle/Tortoise

> phylum Chordata: class Reptilia: order
> Testudines: suborders Cryptodira and Pleurodira:
> Superfamilies Testudinoidea, Trionychoidea,
> Chelonioidea: 200+ species

In Hindu mythology, Tortoise supports the Elephant, who carries the world. The Vedas connect Tortoise with the Lord of the Creatures, who later became an incarnation of Vishnu. In China similar stories of Tortoise supporting the world exist. Thus, it's an auspicious creature that symbolizes water and the feminine principle. Polynesians believe the ocean god can incarnate as a turtle. Sumerians held it sacred to Ea-Oannes, Greeks to Aphrodite, and Romans with Venus. And thanks to the story of the tortoise and the hare, this creature also represents overcoming, tenacity, and steadiness in the face of adversity.

Whale

> phylum Chordata: class Mammalia: order
> Cetacea: suborder Mysticeti (baleen whales)
> 11 species in six genera in four families: suborder
> Odontoceti (toothed whales) 68 species in
> 34 genera in nine families (includes the porpoises
> and dolphins)

In Russia, Arabia, and some Slavic and Arctic regions the supportive earth Tortoise is replaced by a Whale who causes earthquakes when it shakes its tail. Most commonly the symbolism of this creature deals with death and rebirth as well as the power of the Water Element. Norse people feel whales have magickal power, and in Polynesia whales can be manifestations of Ocean gods.

Wolf

> phylum Chordata: class Mammalia: order Carnivora: family Canidae: four species in two genera

Wolves are fiercely protective and have, at times, been considered guides for the dead in the afterlife. In Greco-Roman tradition wolves are associated with Apollo, Ares, Silvanus, and Mars. Celtic and Irish mythology portray the wolf in a good light, as a helpful animal often associated with deitites and heroes of this region, and in Native American custom Wolf is a pathfinder, teacher, and very loyal to those with whom it associates.

Scientific Groupings, Classes, and Subclasses

Phylum Chordata (L. *chorda*, "cord")

Group Craniata

Subphylum Vertebrata (L. *verebratus*, "backboned")
> Bony or cartilaginous vertebrae surrounding spinal cord; notochord in all embryonic stages, persisting in some fish; also may be divided into two groups (superclasses) according to presence of jaws.

Superclass Gnathostomata (Greek *gnathos*, "jaw" + *stoma*, "mouth")
> Jawed fishes, all tetrapods (With jaws and [usually] paired appendages)

Class Chondrichthyes (Gr. *chondros*, "cartilage" + *ichthys*, "a fish")
    sharks, skates, rays, chimaeras

Class Osteichthyes (Gr. *osteon*, "bone" + *ichthys*, "a fish")
    bony fishes

Class Amphibia (Gr. *amphi*, "both or double" + *bios*, "life")
    amphibians

Class Reptilia (L. *repere*, "to creep")
    reptiles

Class Aves (L. pl. of *avis*, "bird")
    birds
    Grouped into 170 families, made up of about 27 orders of living birds (of which 20 orders are represented by North American species) and a few fossil orders. More than 8,600 species and many subspecies. Four of the orders are classified as **ratite**, or flightless birds. The remaining orders are the **carinate**, or birds with a keeled sternum.
        Subclass Archaeornithes (Gr. *archaios*, "ancient" + *ornis, ornithos*, "bird")
            fossil birds
        Subclass Neornithes (Gr. *neos*, "new" + *ornis*, "bird")
            modern birds
                Category
                    Long-legged waders
                        bitterns
                        cranes
                        flamingos
                        herons, egrets
                        ibises
                        limpkins
                        spoonbills
                        storks

Gull-like birds
    frigatebirds
    gannets, boobies
    gulls
    shearwaters
    skimmers
    skuas, jaegers
    storm-petrels
    terns
    tropicbirds

Upright-perching waterbirds
    auks, murres, puffins
    anhingas
    cormorants

Duck-like Birds
    coots
    diving ducks
    geese
    grebes
    loons
    mergansers
    pelicans
    stiff-tailed ducks
    surface-feeding ducks
    swans
    whistling-ducks

Sandpiper-like birds
    avocets, stilts
    oystercatchers
    phalatropes
    plovers, turnstones
    sandpipers

Chicken-like marsh birds
    gallinules
    jacanas
    rails

Upland ground birds
    chachalacas
    goatsuckers
    grouse
    nightjars, nighthawks, whip-poor-wills
    quails, partridges, pheasants
    roadrunners
    snipes, woodcocks
    turkeys

Owls
    barn owls
    true owls

Hawk-like birds
    caracaras
    eagles
    falcons
    harriers
    hawks
    kites
    ospreys
    vultures

Pigeon-like birds
    pigeons, doves

Swallow-like birds
    swallows
    swifts

Tree-clinging birds
    creepers
    nuthatches
    woodpeckers

Perching birds
    becards
    bulbuls
    buntings, finches, sparrows
    cardinals, grosbeaks
    crows
    cuckoos
    flycatchers
    gnatcatchers, kinglets
    hummingbirds
    jays, magpies
    kingfishers
    larks
    meadowlarks
    mockingbirds, thrashers
    orioles, blackbirds
    parrots
    pipits
    shrikes
    starlings
    tanagers
    thrushes
    titmice
    vireos
    waxwings
    weaver finches
    wood warblers
    wrens

Class Mammalia (L. *mamma*, "breast")
  mammals

      Subclass Prototheria (Gr. *protos,* "first" + *ther*, "wild animal")
        The egg-laying mammals

      Subclass Theria (Gr. *ther*, "wild animal")
        Infraclass Metatheria (Gr. *meta*, "after" + *ther*, "wild animal")
          The marsupial mammals
            Order Marsupialia (Gr. *marsypion*, "little pouch")

        Infraclass Eutheria (Gr. *eu*, "true" + *ther*, "wild animal")
          The placental mammals
            Order Edentata (L. *edentatus*, "toothless")
            29 species including anteaters, armadillos, and sloths

            Order Pholidota (Gr. *pholis*, "horny scale")
            One genus and seven species including pangolins

            Order Macroscelidea (Gr. *makros*, "large" + *skelos*, "leg")
            15 species including elephant shrews

            Order Lagomorpha (Gr. *lagos*, "hare" + *morphe*, "form")
            54 species including rabbits and hares

Order Rodentia (L. *rodere*, to gnaw)
Comprises nearly 40 percent of all
mammalian species. Many families
comprising 1591 species

Order Insectivora (L. *insectum*, "an
insect" + *vorare*, "to devour")
343 species including shrews, hedgehogs,
tenrecs, and moles

Order Carnivora (L. *caro*, "flesh"
+ *vorare*, "to devour")
240 species including dogs, wolves, cats,
bears, and weasels

> Canidae (the dog family)
> dogs, wolves, foxes, and
> coyotes

> Felidae (the cat family)
> domestic cats, tigers, lions,
> cougars, and lynxes

> Ursidae (the bear family)
> bears

> Mustelidae (the fur-bearing
> family)
> martens, skunks, weasels,
> badgers, minks, otters,
> wolverines

Order Pinnipedia (L. *pinna*, "feather"
+ *ped*, "foot")
34 species including sea lions, seals, and
walruses

Order Scandentia (L. *scandentis*, "climbing")
16 species including tree shrews

Order Dermoptera (Gr. *derma*, "skin" + *pteron*, "wing")
two species including flying lemurs

Order Chiroptera (Gr. *cheir*, "hand" + *pteron*, "wing")
Many families and 950 species including bat

Order Primates (L. *prima*, "first")
179 species including lemurs, monkeys, apes, humans, and others

> Suborder Prosimii (Gr. *pro*, "before" +*imia*, "ape") includes lemurs, tree shrews, tarsiers, lorises, and pottos

> Suborder Anthropoidea (Gr. *anthropos*, "man") includes monkeys, gibbons, apes, and humans

>> Superfamily Ceboidea (Gr. *kebos*, "long-tailed monkey")
>> New World monkeys

>> Superfamily Cercopithecoidea (Gr. *kerkos*, "tail" + *pithekos*, "monkey")
>> Old World monkeys

Superfamily Hominoidea (L. *homo, hominis,* "man")

Family Pongidae higher apes gibbon, orangutan, chimpanzee, and gorilla

Family Homindae Modern man *(Homo sapiens)*

Order Cetacea (L. *cetus,* "whale") 76 species including whales, dolphins and porpoises

Order Sirenia (Gr. *seiren,* "sea nymph") four species including sea cows and manatees

Order Proboscidea (Gr. *proboski,* "elephant's trunk," from *pro,* "before" + *boskein,* "to feed") two species including elephants

Order Hyracoidea (Gr. *hyrax,* "shrew") five species including hyraxes (coneys)

Order Perissodactyla (Gr. *perissos,* "odd" + *dactylos,* "toe") 17 species including horses, asses, zebras, tapirs, and rhinoceroses

Order Artiodactyla (Gr. *artios,* "even" + *daktylos,* "toe") Nine living families and 184 species including swine, camels, deer, hippopotamuses, antelopes, cattle, sheep, and goats

Suborder Suina
pigs, peccaries, hippopotamuses

Suborder Tylopoda
camels

Suborder Ruminantia
deer, giraffes, sheep, cattle, etc.

Order Tubulidentata (L. *tubulus*, "tube"
+ *dens*, "tooth")
One species including aardvark (Dutch
for "earth pig")

Select Bibliography

Aldington, Richard, translator. *New Larousse Encyclopedia of Mythology*. Hamlyn Publishing Group Limited, 1968.

Andrews, Ted. *Animal Speak*. St. Paul, Minn.: Llewellyn Publications, 1993.

Animals of the World. American Museum of Natural History. 1917. The University Society Inc. reprinted in 1952 by Garden City Books, N.Y.

Black, William George. *Folk Medicine*. Burt Franklin, 1970.

Booth, Ernest S. *How to Know the Mammals*, 3d ed., Iowa: Wm. C. Brown Company Publishers, 1971.

Bull, John and John Farrand, Jr. *The Audubon Society Field Guide to North American Birds, Eastern Region*. The American Museum of Natural History: Alfred A. Knopf, Inc., 1977.

Cochrane, Amanda and Karena Callen. *Dolphins and Their Power to Heal*. Healing Arts Press, 1992.

Colinvaux, Paul. *Ecology*. New York: John Wiley & Sons, Inc., 1986

Conant, Roger. *A Field Guide to Reptiles and Amphibians of Eastern and Central North America*, 2d ed., Boston: Houghton Mifflin Company, 1975.

Cooper, JC. *Symbolic & Mythological Animals*. Aquarian Press, 1992.

Funk & Wagnalls New Encyclopedia. MCMLXXI. N.Y.: Funk & Wagnalls, Inc.

Harper & Row's Complete Field Guide to North American Wildlife; Eastern Edition. Harper & Row, Publishers, Inc., 1981.

Harper & Row's Complete Field Guide to North American Wildlife; Western Edition. Harper & Row, Publishers, Inc., 1981.

Hickman, Cleveland P., Jr., Larry S. Roberts, Frances M. Hickman. *Integrated Principles of Zoology,* 8th ed.,. Mo.: Times Mirror/Mosby College Publishing, 1988.

Jaques, H.E. *Living Things: How to Know Them.* Iowa: Wm. C. Brown Co. Publishers, 1947.

Leach, Maria, ed. *Standard Dictionary of Folklore, Mythology & Legend.* Calif.: Harper San Francisco, 1972.

Loewe, Michael and Carment Blacker, eds. *Oracles and Divination.* Shambhala, 1981.

Lum, Peter. *Fabulous Beasts.* Pantheon Books, Inc., 1951.

Lurker, Manfred. *Gods and Goddesses, Devils & Demons.* Routledge & Kegan Paul Ltd., 1987.

McCutcheon, Marc. *Roget's Super Thesaurus.* Ohio: Writer's Digest Books, 1995.

Mech, L. David. *The Way of the Wolf.* Voyageur Press, Inc., 1991.

Milne, Lorus and Margery. *The Audubon Society Field Guide to North American Insects & Spiders.* University of New Hampshire: Alfred A. Knopf, Inc., 1980.

Mochi, Ugo and T. Donald Carter. *Hoofed Mammals of the World.* Charles Scribner's Sons, 1971.

The Hunter's Field Guide to the Game Birds and Animals of North America. Robert Elman. 1982. Alfred A. Knopf, Inc.

The Tormont Webster's Illustrated Encyclopedic Dictionary. Canada: Tormont Publications Inc., 1990.

The University of Michigan, Museum of Zoology Website *www.ummz.lsa.umich.edu*

The World Encyclopedia of Animals. N.Y.: Funk & Wagnalls, 1972.

Walker, Barbara. *Women's Dictionary of Symbols & Sacred Objects.* Harper & Row Publishers, 1988.

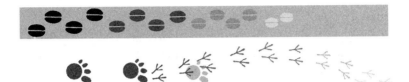

Index

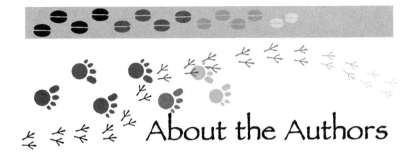

About the Authors

Patricia Telesco has authored more than 50 metaphysical books, including *Money Magick*, *An Enchanted Life*, *Exploring Candle Magick*, *Gardening with the Goddess*, *A Witch's Beverages and Brews*, and *Wicca 2000*. She travels twice a month giving lectures and workshops, and has a strong presence on the Internet through her home page, *www.loresinger.com*. Her current projects include supporting Pagan land funds. Patricia maintains a strong, visible presence in metaphysical journals and Internet sites, where she is a respected and frequent contributor.

Elaine "Rowan" Hall describes herself as an eclectic, pragmatic, scientific Pagan. An active member of the Neo-Pagan community since 1993, she has a deep love and commitment toward those who seek deep spiritual understanding. Rowan and her family (including two German shepherds, a Great Pyreneese, a damn-near-perfect husband, and two awesome teenage daughters) reside in the state of Alaska.